Calvin's Journey to Another World

M. A. FLOYD

Dedication

To my little buddy, Montana, who had shown me nothing but love.

Contents

Chapter One
Calvin Johnson

Calvin Johnson, a 20-year-old Uber driver, is finally heading home after a long day. After finishing his shifts, he would usually head to his night classes, where he was working on his degree. As a student, Calvin is pursuing a degree in Business Administration with a concentration in Entrepreneurship. While his coursework provides the foundational knowledge, it's his part-time job as an Uber driver that adds a layer of practical insight and entrepreneurial skills to his education. Driving for Uber has turned into more than just a way to earn extra income — it's an unexpected but valuable extension of his studies.

Through daily interactions with passengers, Calvin has gained first-hand exposure to a variety of industries, business practices, and personal stories that enrich his understanding of business dynamics. Many of his passengers are professionals in diverse fields — ranging from tech entrepreneurs and corporate executives to small business owners. These chance encounters often turn into impromptu networking opportunities, where he can ask questions about running a business, market trends, and the realities of entrepreneurship.

One particularly insightful experience was when he had a conversation with a seasoned businessman, who, over the course of a 30-minute ride, shared valuable advice on scaling a startup, managing cash flow, and navigating the challenges of customer acquisition. The businessman also spoke candidly about mistakes made along the way, offering Calvin the type of practical, real-world wisdom that textbooks simply can't replicate.

This exposure has influenced Calvin's academic focus. In class, he applies these real-world insights to his assignments, case studies, and even group projects. His experience as an Uber driver has helped him see business concepts in action, making theoretical ideas feel more tangible. For example, when studying marketing principles, he finds himself considering how Uber's dynamic pricing model mirrors the strategies discussed in his coursework about supply and demand, customer behavior, and pricing elasticity.

Moreover, the job has also helped him refine his interpersonal and communication skills — essential attributes for any entrepreneur. As an Uber driver, he's constantly engaging with new people, adapting to different personalities, and learning how to make connections quickly. These soft skills are invaluable in the world of business, where networking and building rapport can lead to opportunities and collaborations.

In essence, Calvin views his time as an Uber driver not just as a side hustle, but as an immersive, living case study that complements his business education. It's giving him a front-row seat to the day-to-day realities of running a service-based business, learning how to manage customer satisfaction, and discovering innovative ways to solve problems on the fly. His job as an Uber driver, far from being a distraction from his studies, has become a vital part of his educational journey.

This approach shows how his job serves as a bridge between classroom knowledge and real-world experience, enriching his degree while building practical skills.

Balancing school and driving wasn't easy, but he was determined to make it work. Early mornings were often spent in lectures, soaking in business theories and strategies that would one day fuel his own entrepreneurial ambitions. By afternoon, he was behind the wheel of his Uber, navigating the busy streets, each trip offering its own unique lessons. He had learned to manage his time with precision—juggling coursework, late-night study sessions, and weekend driving shifts. It wasn't always glamorous, but he was committed to both his education and his financial independence.

As he drives through the familiar streets, he reflects on his day. The hum of the car, the rhythmic sound of tires on pavement, gives him time to think. Most of the time, it's a meditative experience, a few hours away from the chaos of assignments, deadlines, and exams. He recalls the passengers he met that day: the corporate lawyer on her way to a meeting who shared advice on navigating the legalities of starting a business; the startup founder who spoke about the importance of failing fast and pivoting when necessary. Each conversation, no matter how brief, feels like another valuable nugget of wisdom that enriches his understanding of the business world.

Then there were the laughs—those moments when passengers let their guard down and shared stories or jokes, turning an otherwise routine ride into something memorable. A funny encounter with a group of college students on their way to a party, or an elderly couple reminiscing, always reminded him that the human connection was as important as the financial or educational value he gained from his job. Those moments were the highlights of his day, offering a brief escape from the pressures of schoolwork while also reinforcing the importance of customer relations and empathy, both essential skills in any business.

But of course, not every ride was smooth sailing. There were the tough rides too — unpredictable traffic, difficult passengers, and the occasional mechanical issue that had him pulling over to the side of the road, trying to solve the problem before it derailed his entire shift. Those tough moments tested his patience and problem-solving skills, but each time, he learned how to manage stress and stay calm under pressure, a trait he knew would serve him well when running his own company someday.

Through it all, he found balance. The grind of school and the challenges of driving had become a rhythm in his life. The ups and downs, the lessons learned from both the classroom and the driver's seat, were shaping him into someone who understood the value of hard work, resilience, and adaptability. It wasn't always easy, but he never doubted that every mile he drove, every passenger he met, and every piece of business knowledge he absorbed in class were all steps forward on his journey toward becoming an entrepreneur. This version emphasizes the balance between the challenges and the personal growth that comes from juggling both school and a side hustle, highlighting how each experience is contributing to his development in ways both big and small.

Pulling into his parking stall, he feels a mix of exhaustion and satisfaction. The hum of the engine fades, and he's grateful for the small moments, like the conversations he had and the people he met. Stepping out of the car, he stretches and takes a deep breath, ready to unwind before diving back into his studies.

Standing at his front door fishing for his house key that he keeps on a separate key chain. In his thoughts, he is telling himself I am so glad to be home. "Meanwhile, inside, waiting to welcome him home was his dog, Montana…" a small black and white Boston Terrier. Calvin's life hasn't always been about business degrees and driving around town. A few years ago, in the middle of a particularly stressful semester, he found himself in need of some comfort, something to ground him amidst the grind of schoolwork and late-night study sessions. That's when he stumbled upon Montana wasn't just any dog — he was a rescue pup that Calvin's mother had found at a local animal shelter. Calvin hadn't been planning on adopting a dog, especially with his already hectic schedule. Between his demanding coursework, late-night study sessions, and long hours as an Uber driver, he wasn't sure he could take on the responsibility. But when his mom brought Montana home one weekend, Calvin couldn't resist.

At first, he was unsure about the idea. He wasn't sure how he'd fit in with the additional responsibility. Montana had been abandoned as a puppy, but his eager eyes and wagging tail spoke volumes about his resilience and trust in people. There was something about his playful energy and unconditional affection that made it impossible to turn away. After a few visits to the shelter and spending some time with Montana, Calvin knew that this was more than just a fleeting feeling.

He decided to adopt him, and from that moment on, Montana became an inseparable part of his life. Over the past two years, Montana had gone from being just another responsibility to a constant companion and source of joy. Their bond deepened with each passing day, and the routines they shared—morning walks before class or quiet evenings at home—became some of the most cherished moments of Calvin's day.

Though balancing school, work, and dog ownership wasn't always easy, Montana made it worth it. The energy Montana brought into Calvin's life was a perfect counterbalance to the stress of his busy schedule. On days when Calvin felt worn out from long driving shifts or a difficult exam, coming home to Montana's excited greeting and wagging tail felt like a fresh start. It was as if Montana knew exactly how to lift his spirits, just by being there.

As much as Montana relied on Calvin, it was clear that Calvin depended on him, too. The bond they shared gave Calvin the motivation to keep going—even when the balance between school, work, and personal life seemed impossible. And when things got tough, it was Montana who kept him grounded, a reminder that no matter how busy life got, there was always room for a little love and companionship.

"Calvin slips the key into the lock and unlocks the hatch, and the sound triggers Montana – who now knows that his owner will be walking in any moment. He opens the door and is immediately welcomed by Montana. Montana happily starts running in circles with the joy of his owner whose home. Calvin bends down to pet Montana but instead, Montana licks Calvin all over his face. Calvin chuckles as he wrestles with Montana, the little Boston Terrier's enthusiasm infectious. "Hey boy, I'm happy to be home too!" he exclaims, scratching behind Montana's ears while trying to catch his breath from the doggy love attack. As he gets to his feet, he notices the note from Shawn. "Vet appointment, huh?" he mutters, picking it up. Reading the message, a mix of concern and guilt washes over him. He has been giving Montana little scraps from his meals—who could resist those big, soulful eyes? Every time Calvin sat down to eat, he felt a pang of guilt when Montana would watch him with that hopeful gaze, tail thumping softly against the floor.

"I know, I know, you want some too," Calvin would often say, chuckling as he tossed a small piece of chicken or a leftover veggie into Montana's eager mouth. It was hard to say no to such enthusiasm, but he also knew it wasn't the healthiest choice for his little buddy.

"Guess it's time to switch things up, huh?" He realizes he needs to be more disciplined about Montana's diet. "No more table scraps for you," he says, scratching Montana behind the ears as the dog gazes up at him.

Calvin drops his keys on the table, kicks off his shoes, and takes off his coat. In the background, he hears a soft sound of thunder. Calvin shuffles into the kitchen and retrieves a Hungry Man frozen meal from the fridge. He peels off the plastic cover and places the tray inside, setting the timer for a few minutes. The familiar hum of the microwave provides a comforting background noise while heating up, he heads to the living room to grab his TV tray from beside the TV stand.

"Time for some serious relaxation," he says to himself, a smile creeping across his face as he turns on the television. The opening notes of "The Wizard of Oz" fill the room, instantly transporting him back to his childhood. He remembers watching it with his family, the bright colors and fantastical adventures sparking his imagination.

With the microwave ding to signal that his meal is ready, Calvin makes his way back to the kitchen. He carefully takes out the steaming tray and sets it on the TV tray in front of him. As he settles down on the couch, he cannot help but feel a wave of nostalgia wash over him.

"Man, I miss my mom's cooking," he murmurs, taking his first bite of the meal. It isn't quite the same, but it is comforting.

As the movie plays on, he finds himself getting lost in the story, the iconic characters bringing a sense of joy that feels exactly right on Thanksgiving. The warmth of the couch and the smell of his meal make everything feel cozy. He takes another bite and glances over at Montana, who is nestled comfortably on his bed, watching Calvin with curious eyes.

"This is the life, right?" Calvin says, chuckling as he takes another forkful. With the familiar adventure of Dorothy and her friends unfolding on screen, he feels content and grateful for the little things that make evenings like this special.

Calvin feels the warmth of the couch wrap around him as he closes his eyes, the familiar melodies of "The Wizard of Oz" softly playing in the background. The turkey's effects are slow but gentle, lulling him into a light doze. He drifts off, the colorful scenes of Oz fading into dreams.

Meanwhile, Montana, curious and slightly impatient, eyes the TV tray. With Calvin sprawled comfortably on the couch, the tempting remnants of the meal seem just out of reach. He tries to nudge the tray with his nose, but it doesn't budge. Frustrated, he starts to whine softly, then shifts to a series of barks that grow louder, his little paws dancing in anticipation.

After what felt like several hours, Calvin is jolted awake by the sound of Montana barking insistently. Blinking into the dim light of the living room, he sits up, disoriented. "What's going on, buddy?" he mumbles, glancing at the TV where the credits are now rolling.

Montana looks up at him, tail wagging furiously, clearly excited but also slightly annoyed at being ignored. "Okay, okay, I get it!" Calvin laughs, rubbing the sleep from his eyes. He realizes he must have dozed off longer than he intended.

"Are you hungry?" he asks, knowing exactly what the answer will be. Montana barks again, more emphatically this time, his eyes wide and pleading.

Calvin pushes himself off the couch, still a little groggy but eager to get his little buddy fed. He stretches his arms and makes his way to the kitchen, glancing back at Montana, who is watching him with hopeful eyes. "Alright, buddy, let's get you something to eat," he says with a smile.

He opens the pantry and scans the shelves, but his heart sinks when he realizes they are out of dog food. "Uh-oh, looks like I really dropped the ball this time," he mutters, feeling a pang of guilt. Montana tilts his head as if he understands.

Calvin quickly decides that a trip to the store is necessary. "Hold on, boy, I'll be right back," he reassures Montana, who wags his tail in anticipation.

Calvin pauses, realizing he has forgotten to restock Montana's food. "Oh man, I should've checked earlier," he says, feeling a twinge of guilt as he makes his way back into the living room to get ready to step out.

Chapter Two
Trip to the Store

"All right, buddy, let me make a quick trip to the store," Calvin says, giving Montana a reassuring pat. The little dog perks up as if he understands that food is on the horizon. Calvin grabs his raincoat, slips on his shoes, and picks up his cell phone and car keys. He smiles glancing back at Montana, who wags his tail with excitement.

Calvin tells Montana, "Hold on, boy, I'll be right back," he reassures Montana.

After checking to make sure he has everything, he opens the door and steps outside, locking it behind him. The soft sound of rain can be heard as he makes his way down the hallway. The familiarity of the sound feels comforting.

Calvin walks quickly toward the parking lot, the drizzle barely bothers him as he thinks about what treats to get for Montana. "Maybe some new flavors?" he ponders, a smile creeping back to his face at the thought of his little buddy's excitement.

As he reaches his car and climbs inside, he glances back at the building, thinking about how much he loves coming home to Montana's enthusiastic welcome. "Just a quick trip, and then we can have a cozy night in," he promises, starting the engine and pulling out into the rain-slicked road. The adventure of the evening is just beginning, and he feels ready for whatever comes next.

Chapter Three
Mom's Call

Suddenly Calvin's phone begins to ring. He takes his phone out of his slightly wet pocket and sees that it's his mother calling him. A smile spreads across his face as he swipes to answer. "Hey, Mom!" he says, his voice brightening.

"Hi, sweetie! Happy Thanksgiving! How's everything going?" she asks, her warm tone instantly makes him feel at home, even from a distance.

"Happy Thanksgiving, Mom!" Calvin replies, a smile spreading across his face. "Everything's good! Just heading to the store. I realized I forgot to restock Montana's food, so I need to make a quick run."

"So, Mom, who else is there with you?" Calvin asks, curious about the family gathering.

"Your sister and her kids are here! I also invited the Stevens and their daughter. You know she's single," his mom continues, a teasing tone in her voice.

Calvin chuckles, rolling his eyes playfully. "Oh, Mom, not this again! I'm just trying to focus on school and work right now.

Calvin smiles as he switches the conversation back to his Mom and the grandkids. "So, how are the kids doing? Are they excited for the holidays?" he asks, genuinely curious.

"They're all running around like little tornadoes! It's a bit hectic but fun, but you know how it gets — noisy everywhere!" she laughs. "Your sister helped a lot in the kitchen," she explains. "We've got turkey, stuffing, and of course, your favorite — pumpkin pie!"

"Sounds like a perfect Thanksgiving," Calvin says, smiling at the thought of it. "I wish I could be there to help out. Or at least snag a slice of that pie."

"We'll save you some, I promise!" she assures him. "Just don't forget to call later and tell me all about your day."

"Definitely, Mom. I'll catch up with you later," Calvin says, realizing how much he misses being with his family. "Love you!"

"Love you too, honey!" she replies before hanging up. As he continues driving, he feels a mix of nostalgia and appreciation for his family, reminding him of the importance of these connections, even from afar.

The rain pours in sheets as Calvin drives, and the sound of heavy drops splattering against the windshield echoes in the car. He turns on the wiper blades full blast, straining to see through the deluge. As he navigates through the streets, he makes a left onto Michael's Street, heading toward West Hills.

Chapter Four
The Crash

Approaching a traffic light, in the heavy rain, Calvin notices it has just turned from green to red. He stops at the signal, the sound of raindrops tapping against the windshield creating a soothing rhythm. As he sits there, he watches the droplets race down the glass, momentarily lost in thought.

The city is a blur of lights and reflections, the streetlamps casting a warm glow through the downpour. He glances in the rearview mirror, noticing the cars behind him slowing to a stop as well. "Just another rainy night in the city," he murmurs, tapping his fingers on the steering wheel.

As he waits for the light to change, his mind drifts back to his conversation with his mom. He smiles at the thought of the family Thanksgiving gathering—laughter, good food, and the warmth of being with loved ones. It makes him wish he could be there, but he is grateful for the technology that allows him to stay connected.

Just then, a flash of lightning illuminates the sky, followed by a distant rumble of thunder. Calvin instinctively glances up, and as the rain continues to pour, a sense of calm washes over him. "I'll be home soon," he whispers to himself, reminding himself that this is just a temporary phase.

As the traffic signal finally turns green, he eases his foot off the brake and presses on the gas pedal. The rain still pours down and he pulls forward, toward the green light ahead. Suddenly, he sees a flash of movement from the corner of his eye. A car speeds through the intersection, running the red light with reckless abandon. Before Calvin reacts, the vehicle clips the front end of his car, sending him into a wild spin. Time seems to slow down as his heart races, and the world outside becomes a blur of lights and chaos. In that instant, everything feels surreal. The world outside transforms into a blur of colors and shapes, the rain is now a chaotic curtain obscuring his vision.

Calvin's phone flies from its holder, spinning through the air like a projectile, and for a split second, everything moves in slow motion. It feels as if he is caught in a tornado, just like Dorothy in his favorite movie, "The Wizard of Oz."

The slick road makes it nearly impossible to regain control, as the car spins around, and around. A sudden impact hit the car with such forces that Calvin feels the sharp impact to his head as he hit the steering wheel. A jolt of pain courses through him, and in that moment, darkness takes over as he slumps forward, unconscious.

The world fades away, silence and the sound of rain pounding against metal. It feels like a dream or a nightmare that he cannot escape from - the chaos of the accident.

Chapter Five
Aftermath

Calvin slowly stabilizes himself, blinking against the bright light streaming through the shattered windshield. As he tries to sit up, the force of the crash hits him, reminding him of how disoriented everything feels. He squints at the sunlight, trying to make sense of his surroundings. The broken glass crunches under him, a stark reminder of the accident. He reaches for the door handle, eager to escape the confines of the car and assess the situation. "Come on," he mutters, but the door won't budge. He grits his teeth and pushes with all his might, finally feeling it gives way.

As the door swings open, Calvin steps outside, the sunlight blinds him momentarily. He takes a few cautious steps back, trying to regain his bearings, and is surprised to see that the ground is yellow, almost like a golden hue. Confused, he looks around, taking in a field of trees stretching out for miles. It feels surreal like he has somehow been transported to another world.

The trees tower above him, their leaves shimmering in the bright light, creating a canopy that danced with shades of gold and green. Calvin rubs his eyes, hoping to clear the fog from his mind, but the vibrant scenery remains unchanged. It is a stark contrast to the chaos of the accident, and a wave of disorientation washes over him. His heart races as he walks around to the front of the car, anxious to assess the damage.

To his horror, he realizes he has hit a tree hard. The grill is crumpled, and he can see the radiator fluid slowly spilling out onto the ground. He kneels to get a closer look, noting the busted headlight and flat tire. "Great, just great," he says to himself, running a hand through his hair, feeling the remnants of the crash still weighing heavily on him. He takes a deep breath, trying to calm himself. "Okay, let's think this through. First things first, I need to get a grip." Calvin glances around again, hoping to spot someone for help, or at least get a better idea of where he is. The eerie quiet of the forest feels almost otherworldly, and he can't shake the feeling that he is far from home.

Feeling disoriented and anxious, Calvin climbs back into the car, searching desperately for his phone. He looks between the seats and on the floor, his heart sinks as he rummages through the debris. Just as he is about to give up, he spots it underneath the passenger seat. With a sigh of relief, he grabs the phone and steps back outside. Holding the phone aloft, he scans the area, hoping to catch a signal. He squints at the screen, but it shows no service. Panic begins to creep in. "Come on, please!" he pleads, shaking the phone slightly as if that will help. He turns the phone off and then back on, praying that maybe it will connect. As the phone boots up, he glances around at the endless stretch of trees, feeling a knot tighten in his stomach.

The isolation is unsettling. Suddenly, to Calvin's shock, The apple tree turns toward him and speaks. Calvin falls backwards to the ground as his iphone fell out from his hand. "Of all the places to crash, you had to crash into me! Look at what you did! This will take years to heal!"

The tree's bark creaks with anger, its branches shaking as if in distress. In the background, the other apple trees murmur in hushed tones, their voices a soft rustle of leaves, expressing their disbelief and concern at the commotion. "How could this happen?" one tree whispered. "A human in the grove?"

Gathering his composure, he gets back on his feet and manages to ask, "You can speak?"

"Of course!" the apple tree replies, "Now, can you get this trap off me?" Frustration is evident in its tone. Calvin is eager to ask more questions, but time is of the essence. He dashes back to his car, hoping it will start and allow him to move it away from the tree. He turns the ignition, but the engine sputters and fails to catch. "Great," he mutters, feeling the pressure of the situation. He looks back at the tree, which is clearly in pain.

"I'll try to push it off you, sir or miss?"

"Just hurry up!" the tree urges, its branches swaying slightly as if in distress. Calvin takes a deep breath, hoping to muster enough strength to push the car off the tree. The situation feels surreal, but the urgency courses through him as he glances at the damage he has caused. He puts the car in neutral, gritting his teeth as he pushes against the front bumper, hoping to unhook it from the tree. He leans into it, muscles straining, and feels the car shifting. With each push, he can feel the tires starting to roll, the weight of the vehicle moving ever so slightly away from the tree.

"Come on, just a little more," he urges himself, pouring every ounce of strength into the effort. The ground is uneven beneath him, making it more difficult, but he focuses on the tree's relief. He imagines the tree healing, the bark mending as he pushes. Finally, with a grunt, he feels the bumper break free from the trunk. Panting heavily, he steps back and wipes his brow, glancing at the tree.

"Is that better?" he asks, his voice hoarse.

"Yes, much better," the apple tree replies, its tone softer with the sound of relief. "I wish it hadn't come to this." Now, let me recover from this ordeal. And you… be more careful next time!" Calvin nods, still trying to process everything.

"I can't believe I just talked to a tree," he mutters, shaking his head in disbelief. "What's next? A talking squirrel?" Calvin shakes his head in disbelief, still processing the encounter. "I'll try," he promises, glancing at the car that has let him down. "I just hope I can figure out how to get back home." Calvin bends down to pick up his phone from the ground, his heart sinking further when he sees it still showing no sign of a cell connection.

Frustrated, he walks up to the tree. He reaches out his hand to tap the bark of the tree to ask it a question. "Where am I?" In the background, he can hear the other apple trees murmuring softly. "Don't speak to him," one whispers. "He might bring more trouble." Another tree adds, "We can't trust a human. Look what he's done already!" Calvin expresses his frustration to the apple tree, "I can't get a signal to call for a tow."

The great apple tree turns to Calvin and tells him, "You're in Gold Valley Oz," the tree replies curtly.

"Wait, you said Oz?" Calvin repeats, his mind racing with disbelief.

"Yes, and now I don't have time for idle chit-chat," the tree snaps. "I need to heal from what that trap did to my coat. How soon can you get it out of my sight?"

"I'm trying, but my phone isn't working out here!" Calvin shoots back, exasperated. The tree shoots him a mean look and turns its back, clearly annoyed. "I am done with you."

Calvin feels a mix of irritation and sympathy. "Wait! How far is it to the nearest town from here?" he asks, hoping for some clarity.

"The next town is a few hours away," the tree replies, its tone slightly softer now. "But there's a farmhouse east just up the road. The farmer may have a wagon to help remove that nasty trap of yours."

Feeling a surge of hope, Calvin manages to smile a grateful smile. "Thanks for that information about the farmhouse," he says sincerely, even if it feels strange to thank a tree.

He steps back out onto the road, glancing in both directions, trying to figure out which way to go. "Wonder which direction that farmhouse is?" he murmurs to himself, squinting into the distance. After a moment of hesitation, he decides to head east, recalling the tree's earlier advice as he tries to shake off the strange events of the day. With every step, he focuses on reaching the farmhouse and finding a way to get back home.

Chapter Six
Scarecrow

Calvin trudges eastward, the vibrant landscape around him both enchanting and unsettling. The golden hues of the ground contrast sharply with the deep green of the trees, and every rustle of leaves sends a shiver down his spine. The surreal atmosphere makes him question if he is still dreaming.

He glances back at the apple tree, which stands proudly despite the recent encounter. "Thanks for the help!" he called out, half-expecting the tree to respond, but it remained silent, likely too focused on healing.

As he walks, Calvin cannot shake the odd sensation. The trees, though still, seem to lean in closer, their branches whispering secrets he can't quite decipher. He shakes his head, trying to focus on the task at hand. "Just get to the farmhouse," he muttered to himself, picking up his pace.

After what feels like an eternity, Calvin's heart races as he hears the cawing of crows and someone yelling for help. "What the heck is going on?" he thinks, adrenaline kicking in. As he rounds a turn, he stumbles upon a vast field of tall corn plants swaying gently in the breeze. "These corn stalks are huge," he mutters to himself, glancing over to his right. He notices a flock of crows flying erratically above the cornstalks, making a racket as they flap their wings. In their feet, they clutch what looks like a piece of cloth, twisting in the wind. Just as he starts to make sense of it, the crows drop the cloth, only to try again, their frantic movements drawing Calvin's attention. Then he hears the scream again, clearer this time—a cry for help. Without thinking, he bolts toward the sound, sprinting into the cornfield. The tall plants whip against him, smacking his arms and legs as he pushes through the dense foliage.

"Hold on! I'm coming!" he shouts, his voice barely rising above the cacophony of crows. The stalks close in around him, making it hard to see where he is going, but he follows the sound, weaving through the towering corn. As he runs, his mind races with questions. Who was calling for help? What kind of trouble were they in? Each step feels like a leap into the unknown, but he is determined to reach whoever is in need.

As Calvin bursts through the corn stalks, the sound of crows intensifies, their raucous filling the air. He appears in a small clearing, and to his shock, all the crows scatter in various directions, leaving behind a sight that sends a chill down his spine. There, lying on the ground is a scarecrow, its straw spilling out and its clothing tattered and torn. It looks like it had been through a rough ordeal, the fabric worn and battered from the relentless attacks of the crows.

When the scarecrow spots Calvin, it lifts its head slightly, its button eyes wide with desperation. "Please, help me!" it pleads; its voice surprisingly human. Calvin stands frozen, a mix of fear and disbelief washing over him. "What… how are you able to talk?" he stammers, still hesitant to move closer.

"Please! I don't have much time! If those dirty creatures come back, who knows where they'll take me!" The scarecrow's tone is urgent, with panic evident in its voice. Calvin's instincts kick in. "Okay, okay, just hold on!" he says, shaking off his initial fear. He steps forward, kneeling beside the scarecrow. "What can I do?" Push my stuffing back inside me. Calvin quickly moves to help the scarecrow, stuffing hay back into its top and bottom, working to restore its form. He carefully reaches for its left arm, pushing the parts together until the scarecrow is complete once more. "Help me up," the scarecrow says, its voice steadying with newfound strength.

Calvin grasps its arm, lifting it carefully. The scarecrow wobbles at first, struggling to find its balance, but soon gains its composure, standing tall amidst the cornfield. "Thank you for being here at the right place and the right time," the scarecrow says, its button eyes glinting with gratitude. "I thought I was done for!"

Calvin feels a rush of relief. "I'm just glad I could help. Those crows were really after you!" "They can be relentless," the scarecrow replies, brushing itself off. "But now that I'm whole again, I can take care of myself. You've done me a great service."

Calvin smiles, still processing the surreal nature of the situation. "So, what now? Are you going to scare those crows away?"

"Yes, but I can also help you," the scarecrow offers. "Are you lost? I can guide you to the farmhouse. The farmer will help you get back on your way."

"That would be great!" Calvin says, feeling a sense of hope. "Lead the way!"

The scarecrow nods, adjusting its hat back onto its head. "Follow me, then. We'll find that farmhouse together. And don't worry, I'll keep those pesky crows at bay."

With a newfound ally by his side, Calvin followed the scarecrow deeper into the cornfield, feeling a bit more confident about the adventure ahead. Calvin walks alongside the scarecrow, curiosity getting the better of him. "What happened to you?" he asks, genuinely interested. The scarecrow sighs, its voice carrying a hint of melancholy.

"I was up on my post, just watching the view of the cornfield. Everything was peaceful until a strong gust of wind blew me off my perch, slamming me to the ground and splitting me into pieces. That's when those nasty creatures came for me," it explains, glancing back at Calvin with gratitude. "Then you came and rescued me."

"Wow, that sounds rough," Calvin replies, picturing the scarecrow tumbling down from its post. "I can't believe you were left there like that."

"It's not uncommon," the scarecrow says, its tone growing more philosophical. "Life in the fields can be unpredictable. One moment you're standing tall, and the next, you're scattered on the ground. But that's why I appreciate your help so much. It's a reminder that even in the most unexpected situations, someone can come along and make things right."

Calvin nods, feeling a connection to the scarecrow's words. "I guess we all have our moments of being knocked down," he says, reflecting on his own day. "But it's good to know we can get back up with a little help."

"Exactly!" the scarecrow replies, its expression brightening. "And now, together, we can find that farmhouse. Let's not waste any more time."

With renewed purpose, they continue through the cornfield, the scarecrow leading the way while Calvin feels a sense of camaraderie forming with his unusual companion. Walking alongside the scarecrow, Calvin smiles and asks curiously, "What's your name?"

"I'm Hayman," the scarecrow replies with a sly smile as if Calvin has just asked an off-the-wall question. "Though, you could say I'm a bit of a 'hay-filled of a man."

Calvin asks, "So, how long have you been up on your perch before the wind knocked you off?"

Hayman chuckles, the sound like rustling leaves. "Oh, I've been standing here for many seasons — longer than I can count! I lost track of time after the first few years. It's hard to keep a calendar when you're made of straw!"

"Wow, that must be quite a long time," Calvin replies, intrigued. "What's it like watching everything change around you?"

"It's a mix of wonder and melancholy," Hayman says, a sense of nostalgia in his voice as he glances around the grove. "Each scarecrow has a role to play, protecting the crops and keeping the crows at bay. I've seen crops grow and wither, seasons shift from vibrant greens to the starkness of winter. Each change brings its own stories and lessons. The beauty is in the cycles of life — every year brings new growth and new challenges. I'm a guardian of stories." Hayman continues, "You see, I wasn't always the only scarecrow in this grove. Eighty years ago, there was another scarecrow watching over this land — one who stood tall and proud. But over time, his hay dried out and lost its strength. The farmer decided it was time for a change and replaced him with me."

Calvin frowns, feeling a mix of sympathy and curiosity. "That must have been tough for him."

"Eighty years?" Calvin exclaims, impressed. "That's quite a legacy!"

Hayman nods, his expression thoughtful. "Yes, indeed. He watched over this land for nearly a lifetime, and the stories he collected are woven into the very fabric of Gold Valley Oz. Every crow he scared away, every seed he nurtured — those moments shaped this place."

Calvin nods, intrigued. "That sounds kind of lonely, though."

Hayman tilts his head thoughtfully. "At times, it can be. Standing alone in the fields, watching the world go by, it's easy to feel isolated. But I've learned to find joy in the small things — the rustle of the leaves, the sound of the crows in the distance, and seeing the coming and going of creatures. Each day brings something new, and I've come to appreciate the rhythm of life around me."

Calvin nods, understanding. "It sounds like you've found a way to connect with your surroundings, even if it's just you and the land."

Calvin ponders this for a moment, feeling inspired. "That's a beautiful way to look at it, Hayman. Maybe I need to remember that myself."

"Life has its ups and downs," Hayman says wisely. "But it's the connections we make that truly matter. Each person we meet, each story we hear, adds something special to our journey."

As they continue toward the farmhouse, Calvin feels a deeper bond forming with Hayman, grateful for the unexpected friendship in this strange land.

"What is your name, friend?" Hayman asks, turning its button eyes toward Calvin.

"Calvin," he replies with a smile. "It's nice to meet you, Hayman."

"Pleasure's all mine, Calvin!" Hayman says, a hint of cheerfulness in his voice., feeling a little more comfortable. "What part of Gold Valley are you from?"

"Gold Valley?" Calvin echoes, tilting its head in confusion. "Oh? I'm not from here. I live in Los Angeles with my dog, Montana."

"Where is this Los Angeles you speak of? And where is your dog?" Hayman inquires, genuinely curious.

Calvin hesitates, trying to piece together how to explain. He still feels uncertain about how he ended up in this strange place. "Well,

Los Angeles is a big city far from here. It's known for its beaches, movies, and—" He pauses, thinking about Montana. "But my dog is at home, waiting for me to return and feed him."

Hayman's expression softens. "A dog? That sounds wonderful! What's his name?"

"Montana," Calvin replies, a smile creeping onto his face. "He's a little Boston Terrier, full of energy and personality. I miss him already."

"Animals have a special way of filling our lives with joy," Hayman says. "They remind us of the simple pleasures. I can understand why you'd want to get back to him." Hayman nodded knowingly. "I understand the bond one shares with their pets. Animals have a special way of making our lives richer. They bring comfort, joy, and a sense of companionship that's hard to match."

Calvin smiles, "Exactly! Montana always knows how to cheer me up after a long day. He's more than just a pet; he's family."

"That's beautiful," Hayman replies, his button eyes gleaming. "I may be made of straw, but I've seen the love between humans and their animal companions. It's one of the most genuine connections there is."

"I guess it's something we can all relate to, whether we're human or… well, a scarecrow," Calvin says with a chuckle. Calvin takes a deep breath and begins to share his story with Hayman. "I was heading to the store to get dog food for Montana. I'd forgotten to restock, and I feel guilty leaving him without anything to eat."

Hayman nods, his straw face reflecting sympathy. "That's understandable. Our pets rely on us, and it's hard when we feel we've let them down."

"Exactly," Calvin continues. "So, I jumped into my car, juggling my thoughts about school, work, and Montana's needs. That's when things took a turn for the worse."

"What happened?" Hayman asks, genuinely interested.

"A car ran a red light and collided with mine," Calvin says, shaking his head at the memory. "It all happened so fast. I felt the impact, and the next thing I knew, I was waking up here in this strange place."

"That sounds terrifying," Hayman replies, his button eyes wide with concern. "But it seems you found your way to something unexpected."

"Yeah, I didn't expect to end up in Gold Valley Oz," Calvin says, glancing around at the vibrant surroundings. "But now I'm starting to think, is this a dream or a nightmare?"

Hayman chuckles softly, his straw form rustling in the breeze. "That's a common question when you find yourself in a place as unusual as this. It can feel surreal, can't it?"

"Absolutely," Calvin replies, shaking his head in disbelief. "One moment I'm driving to the store, and the next, I'm talking to a scarecrow and apple tree in a magical land. It's hard to wrap my head around it."

Hayman tilts his head, a knowing smile on his face. "It's a lot to take in, for sure. But sometimes, the most extraordinary experiences come from the most ordinary moments. This land has a way of surprising us. Let's take it one step at a time," Hayman says encouragingly. "We'll find a way to help you, and maybe even uncover some valuable lessons along the way."

Calvin feels a wave of gratitude washes over him. "Thanks, Hayman. I really appreciate your support. With a newfound sense of determination, Calvin nods.

"Alright, let's see what adventures await us." Together, they continue toward the farmhouse, ready to embrace whatever Gold Valley has in store.

As the two make their way through the tall corn stalks, Hayman looks at Calvin with a mix of confusion and curiosity. So, Calvin can you explain to me "What is a stoplight? And what is a car?" he asks, tilting his head.

Calvin chuckles at the innocence in Hayman's question. Calvin pulls out his phone from his front pocket. "Let me show you," he says, holding it up to display a picture of his car.

Hayman takes a step back, eyes wide with surprise. "What is that? Is it some kind of wizard magic device?"

Calvin laughs, yet seeing the fear in Hayman's eyes, he quickly reassures him. "No, no, it's not magic, "No, no, it's harmless! It's just technology — like a fancy tool to help me communicate and capture memories. No wizardry involved. It's called a phone."

Intrigued, Hayman moves closer, peering at the small white device. "I've never seen anything like that before."

"It's pretty handy," Calvin explains. "I can use it to call people, send messages, and even take pictures. Yeah, this is an Apple iPhone," Calvin explains. "I've had it for several years now. They have a new model out, but it costs too much."

Calvin continues, "My phone has all the information I need at my fingertips. It's like a lifesaver for me. Like you did for me back there with the crows?"

Hayman asks, his voice filled with understanding. "Not exactly like that, but close enough."

Calvin chuckles. As Hayman inches closer, Calvin scrolls through his pictures, showing him snapshots of people and places.

Hayman's eyes widen in wonder. "You captured all this in such a small frame?"

"Yep! These pictures are of things I love and want to remember," Calvin says, smiling as he pauses at the photo of his mom with Montana. "That's my mom with my dog, Montana." For a moment, Calvin stares at the picture, a warm feeling filling him as he thinks of home. But he quickly snaps back to reality and says to Hayman, "I really need to find that farmhouse so I can get back home."

Hayman nods enthusiastically. "Yes, it's this way! Follow me!" Calvin follows Hayman down the path, feeling hopeful about finding help and getting back to Montana.

Chapter Seven
The Farmhouse

Calvin and Hayman walked side by side through the tall corn stalks, weaving their way toward the farmhouse. The sun begins to peek through the clouds, casting a warm glow over the field.

As they navigate through the dense rows of corn, it feels almost magical, as if the stalks are parting for them. Suddenly, they break through the last line of stalks, and there stands the farmhouse in the distance, its red paint vibrant against the lush greenery.

"There it is!" Hayman exclaims, pointing toward the house. "That's the farmer's place. He should be able to help you."

Calvin squints at the farmhouse, feeling a mix of relief and excitement. "Looks like a classic country home," he says, taking in the sight of the wraparound porch and tall chimney.

As they approach, Calvin notices a few chickens pecking at the ground and a couple of goats wandering around. The atmosphere feels alive and welcoming.

"Do you think the farmer will be there?" Calvin asks, glancing at Hayman.

"Oh, I'm sure he's home," Hayman replies confidently. "He's usually busy tending to the animals or fixing things around the place."

As they reach the front gate, Calvin takes a deep breath, feeling hopeful. "Let's go see if he can help me get my car back on the road."

With Hayman leading the way, they walk up the path toward the farmhouse, ready to face whatever awaits them inside.

As they approach, a sturdy-looking farmer emerges from the barn, wiping his hands on a dirty rag. "Good day!" he calls out, glancing at the two newcomers.

Hayman steps forward, eager to greet the farmer. With his story as to what happen to him today. He leans into the Farmer "Hello! I've got quite the tale for you," he begins. "I was knocked down from my post by a gust of wind, and then those nasty creatures attacked me. Just when I thought I was done for, this boy appeared out of the blue and saved me."

The farmer raises an eyebrow, intrigued. "Is that so? And who might this boy be?"

"This is Calvin," Hayman says, gesturing to him. "He's from a faraway place called Los Angeles."

Calvin waves, feeling a bit shy under the farmer's scrutinizing gaze. "Hi there! Nice to meet you."

The farmer extends his hand, shaking Calvin's firmly. "Pleasure's mine. I appreciate you helping Hayman here. It's not every day a scarecrow gets rescued."

"Sure," Calvin replies, feeling a bit more at ease. "I'm hoping you might be able to help me too. I had a bit of an accident with my car, and I need to figure out how to get it back on the road."

The farmer's expression shifts from curiosity to concern. "An accident, you say? Where is your wagon?"

"It's just down the road, by an apple tree," Calvin explains. "I crashed into it during a storm and ended up here."

The farmer chuckles, wiping his hands again. "Son you've got yourself in a bit of trouble, that apple tree is no ordinary tree. She's got quite a reputation around here for being temperamental. If you bumped into her, you've stirred up a bit of trouble."

Calvin rubs the back of his neck, feeling a wave of guilt. "I didn't mean to! I just crashed into her while trying to get home."

The farmer shakes his head, a smile creeping onto his face. "Well, you'll need to make it up to her somehow, but first things first. Let's look at your wagon. I can help tow it back here and see what's broken."

Calvin feels a little relief. "Thank you! I really appreciate it."

The farmer moves with purpose as he enters the barn, making his way to the strongest horse, a sturdy mare with a shiny coat. He expertly harnesses her to the wagon, tying everything securely.

As he leads the horse and wagon out, Calvin and Hayman stand by, watching with anticipation. The farmer calls out, "This old girl will get the job done. She's strong enough to pull your wagon back without any trouble."

Calvin feels a wave of gratitude. "Thanks! I didn't think I'd find someone to help me so quickly."

"Just part of the job," the farmer replies with a smile. "Now, let's get going. The sooner we can haul your wagon back, the sooner we can figure out what needs fixing."

Calvin nods and climbs onto the wagon, feeling a mix of excitement and nervousness. Hayman hops up beside him, looking eager to help. "This is going to be an adventure!" the scarecrow says, his straw-filled body bouncing slightly as the wagon begins to roll.

As they travel down the path, Mrs. Farmer steps out of the house, her voice cheerful as she calls out, "Honey, who's our guest?"

"It's Hayman and Calvin!" the farmer replies, waving back. Calvin and Hayman both raise their hands in greeting.

Mrs. Farmer smiles and asks, "Where are you going, honey?"

"I'm going down the road to get this young man's wagon," the farmer says with a nod.

Calvin quickly corrects him, "No, sir, it's my car."

"Whatever, son," the farmer chuckles. "Just hop in the back, and we're off."

Turning to his wife, Mr. Farmer says, "Honey, I'll be back for dinner."

Mrs. Farmer then turns her gaze back to Calvin and Hayman. "Maybe your friends would like to stay for dinner?"

The farmer turns around, looking expectantly at them. "Well, fellas, you're more than welcome to stay for dinner."

Hayman responds eagerly, "Sure, we'd like that!"

The farmer grins, turning back to his wife. He yells, "They'd love to join us for dinner!"

"Great!" she replies with a warm smile. "We'll have a feast waiting for you when you return."

Calvin felt a warmth in his chest at the invitation. "Thank you! That sounds wonderful," he says, feeling grateful for their hospitality.

With that, they continue down the road, the promise of a warm meal ahead making the journey even more enjoyable. As they ride along, Calvin feels a sense of belonging in this strange land, comforted by the kindness of the farmer and Hayman's cheerful presence.

The farmer guides the horse down the dirt path, the sound of hooves crunching on gravel creating a steady rhythm. "So, Calvin, tell me more about this Los Angeles place. What's it like?"

As they travel, Calvin begins to share stories of his life back home, feeling more at ease with each word. The journey is an unexpected turn in his day, but with Hayman and the farmer by his side, it feels a little less daunting.

Calvin glances down at the yellow road stretching ahead of them, with piqued curiosity, he asks Hayman "What's up with the yellow road?"

Hayman looks thoughtful, his straw-stuffed body swaying gently as the wagon bumps along. "Oh, that used to be made of bricks—beautiful, yellow bricks. But time and weather have worn them down to what you see today."

Calvin nods, a sense of familiarity washing over him. "That sounds oddly familiar. I feel like I've seen or read something about a road like this before."

Hayman tilts his head, intrigued. "You're not from around here, are you? You've heard tales of the Yellow Brick Road?"

"The Yellow Brick Road?" Calvin echoes, his eyes widening. "Isn't that from The Wizard of Oz?"

Hayman's face lights up. "Exactly! It's the road that leads to Emerald City. Many travelers have followed it in search of their hearts' desires. But now, it's mostly just a memory."

Calvin chuckles, feeling a mix of nostalgia and wonder. "So, I'm on the Yellow Brick Road? That's insane!"

"Indeed!" Hayman replies with a hint of pride in his voice. "And now you're part of the story. Let's see where this road takes you."

As they continue along the winding path, Calvin feels excitement bubbling inside him.

The farmer's voice grows deeper as he begins to share a story passed down from his father through his generations. "You see, this road was created by a great and powerful man," he explains. "He laid the yellow bricks to guide those who were lost to the wonderful land of Oz. But there's more to the tale."

Calvin and Hayman leaned in, intrigued.

The farmer continues, "Rumor has it that, back in the day, there were three girls who grew up together in a small village near here. They were the best of friends, each with their dreams and aspirations. But one day, darkness fell over their village—a powerful witch wanted to control the land and its magic."

"What happened to the girls?" Calvin asks, his heart racing with curiosity.

"The girls tried to stand up to the witch," the farmer replied. "But her magic was strong, and they were separated. Each one was sent off in different directions, lost to the winds of fate. The yellow bricks were meant to help guide lost souls, but the witch twisted the magic of Oz, making it difficult for anyone to find their way."

Hayman adds, "So, the yellow road became a symbol of both hope and danger. Those who wander here seek to find not only their way but also the truth behind the darkness that lingers in the shadows."

Calvin feels a shiver run down his spine. "Did people still search for the girls?"

The farmer nods solemnly. "Many have tried. Some say they can still hear their whispers in the wind, calling for help. It's a reminder that the path to Oz is filled with challenges and mysteries."

As the wagon continues down the road, Calvin cannot help but feel a sense of responsibility. He is part of this tale now, and he wonders what role he may play in uncovering the truth of the past.

The farmer leans in, lowering his voice as if sharing a secret. "And you know, rumor has it that a house fell from the sky and smashed right on top of one of the wicked witches."

Calvin's eyes widen. "Really? A house?"

"Yep," the farmer continues, a twinkle in his eye. "It was a curious event. The story goes that a girl from another land—someone completely unexpected—found her way here, just like you."

Hayman chimes in, "She had a heart full of courage and a desire to return home. With the help of her friends, she not only defeated the wicked witch but also brought hope to the land of Oz."

Calvin feels a surge of connection to the story. "So, the house wasn't just a coincidence; it was part of a bigger tale?"

"Exactly," the farmer says, nodding. "That house was a catalyst, a turning point for Oz. But even with the witch gone, there are still remnants of darkness that linger, waiting for someone brave enough to confront it."

As they continue along the yellow road, Calvin feels a sense of destiny unfolding. "Maybe I'm here for a reason," he muses aloud. "To help uncover the truth and maybe even help those lost girls."

The farmer smiles. "Well, if anyone can do it, I believe it's you, Calvin. You've got the spirit of a true adventurer."

With renewed determination, Calvin looks ahead at the winding path, ready to embrace whatever challenges lie ahead in this strange and magical land.

As they approach the field of apple trees, the air fills with the sound of a woman's voice—sharp and complaining. "Where is that kid? Why isn't this trap gone yet?"

The apple Tree's frustration is palpable as the farmer pulls the wagon closer to the tree. "Hey, hey! I'm here now!" he calls out, trying to sound reassuring.

Calvin looks around, feeling a mix of confusion and amusement at the sight of the grumpy tree. "Please remove this beast!" The tree urges as she shakes her branches with exasperation.

As they come into view, both Hayman and the farmer spot Calvin in the wagon. "Calvin! Is this your car?" Hayman asks, a hint of disbelief in his voice.

Calvin chuckles nervously. "Yeah, it's my car. Kind of a rough day for it, though." He gestures at the battered vehicle that has caused this whole adventure.

The farmer hops down from the wagon and approaches apple tree, a mix of sympathy and authority in his demeanor. "Alright, let's see what we can do to help."

"Finally!" Apple tree exclaims, her branches swaying as she prepares for the rescue. "That trap has been weighing me down!"

Calvin, the farmer and Hayman all work together to carefully lift the heavy trap off apple tree's root that is still tangled in the tree. As they do, the tree lets out a sigh of relief, her leaves shimmering in the sunlight.

"Thank you, thank you!" she says, her voice softer now. "You have no idea how long I've been stuck like that."

Calvin smiles, feeling a sense of camaraderie with the unlikely group. "Glad we could help, at that moment Hayman introduce Calvin to Mrs. Granny Smith Apple Tree. Nice to meet you Mrs. Smith. Again, so sorry for what my car and I did to you, I guess I was at the wrong place at the wrong time."

Mrs. Smith chuckles, a lightness returning to her branches. "Sometimes, the wrong place leads to the right adventure."

As they gather around, Calvin feels a strange connection growing among them. This journey is turning out to be more than just a quest for help; it is becoming something much more.

Hayman and the farmer exchange glances, both intrigued and hesitant as they examine Calvin's car. The farmer scratches his head, eyeing the vehicle's sleek design with a mix of curiosity and caution. "I've never seen anything quite like this," he admits, leaning closer to peer through the window.

Calvin chuckles at their apprehension. "It's just a car, guys. It's meant to get around—just like your wagon."

Hayman steps back, a puzzled expression on his straw-filled face. "But how do you even hook it up? There's no hitch like on the wagon."

The farmer nods, deep in thought. "That's true. We'll need to get creative." He walks around the car, examining it from different angles, while Hayman follows closely, still unsure about the strange machine.

The farmer chuckles confidently, giving Calvin a reassuring nod. "Don't worry, I once hitched three wagons at once when my wife and I moved from the city out to the country. I've got this!"

Calvin feels relieved. "Okay, if you say so! Just let me know if you need me to steer or anything."

With a firm grip on the reins, the farmer coaxes the horse forward, and the wagon creaks into motion. Hayman walks alongside, keeping an eye on the makeshift connection between the car and the wagon.

"See? Easy as pie!" the farmer says, glancing back at Calvin with a grin.

Hayman chats amiably with Mrs. Smith about her bountiful apple harvest. "Those apples look fantastic this year! I can't remember the last time I saw such vibrant colors on a tree."

Mrs. Smith's branches rustle proudly. "Thank you, Hayman! It's been a good season. The rain and sunshine have been just right. My apples are sweeter than ever!

That's when Hayman mentions as he leans into Mrs. Smith casually, "Calvin has a white apple he keeps in his pocket!"

Mrs. Smith's branches quiver with alarm. "What? One of my apples? He must return it at once!" She turns her gaze sharply toward Calvin. "You took one of my apples from my tree? Give it back!"

Calvin, taken aback, raises his hands defensively. "I didn't take anything! It's not an apple; it's my phone!"

Hayman leans in, looking at Calvin's pocket. "But you do have an apple on that thing, right?"

Calvin nods but quickly pulls out his phone to show them. "See? It's just the logo of the company that made it. It's not an actual apple!"

Mrs. Smith frowns, her branches shaking with confusion. "A logo? What kind of trickery is this?"

As Calvin tries to explain, Hayman steps closer. "It's not a trick, Mrs. Smith. This is a device that helps him communicate and capture moments. It's not a piece of fruit!"

Calvin nods fervently. "Exactly! I'm just trying to get back home to my dog, Montana. I promise I didn't mean any harm!"

As Mr. Farmer shouts, "Let go, boys!" Calvin and Hayman jump onto the back of the wagon just in time. They watch as Mrs. Smith flails her branches, her leaves rustling in a furious dance.

"Drive! Drive!" Calvin urges, feeling a mix of excitement and fear.

Mr. Farmer chuckles, urging the horse forward. "Don't worry, boys. She's all bark and no bite!"

As the wagon rolls away, Hayman waves back at Mrs. Smith. "Thanks for the apples!" he calls, trying to lighten the mood.

Calvin laughs nervously. "I hope she doesn't follow us!"

The farmer glances back, grinning. "She's too busy fussing over her trees to bother with us now."

As they make their way down the winding road, the landscape of Gold Valley Oz unfolds before them, vibrant and full of life. Calvin can't help but feel a sense of adventure, despite the oddness of the day. "So, what's next?" he asks, eager to know more about this strange land.

Hayman looks at Calvin with a twinkle in his eye. "Well, now that you've met Mrs. Smith, maybe you'll want to visit some other interesting folks around here!"

Mr. Farmer nods. "You're in for a wild ride, son. Oz has many surprises in store for you!"

Calvin asks the farmer as they head back to the farm. Do you think you can fix my car?

Mr. Farmer scratches his chin, deep in thought. "Well, I might not have what you need, but I can't leave you stranded out here.

Mrs. Farmer comes walking out of the house, her apron still dusted with flour, and greets them warmly. "Dinner is ready! You boys go and wash up, and I'll meet you in the dining room."

Calvin and Mr. Farmer exchange appreciative smiles before heading toward the outdoor sink. As they wash their hands, Calvin can't help but feel a sense of comfort in this strange place.

Once they are clean, they follow the delightful aroma wafting from the kitchen. The dining room is quaint, with a wooden table set for three, surrounded by warm, homey decor.

Mrs. Farmer soon enters, carrying a steaming platter of roasted chicken, golden brown and succulent. "I hope you're hungry!" she says cheerfully as she sets the dish down in the center of the table.

Calvin's mouth waters as she begins serving the chicken along with generous helpings of mashed potatoes, green peas, and freshly baked rolls. The comforting smell reminds him of home, and he feels a pang of nostalgia.

"Go ahead, help yourselves," Mrs. Farmer encourages.

As they dig into the meal, Calvin shares bits of his story, sharing a little bit about himself with the warm strangers who were so kind to help him and to provide a meal for him. The farmers listen intently, nodding, and expressing disbelief.

When they finish eating, Mrs. Farmer leans back in her chair, wiping her hands on her apron. "So, Calvin, where are you from?"

"Los Angeles," he replies, glancing around the table. "And honestly, I'm not sure how I got here. I just want to go back home to my dog, Montana, and let my mom know I'm okay."

"Oh dear," Mrs. Farmer says, concern etched on her face. "I bet she's worried sick about you."

Calvin turns to Mr. Farmer, a hopeful expression on his face. "Can you help me fix my car?"

Mr. Farmer shakes his head. "I'm not sure how to fix it, son. I don't have much in my barn that can get it working again."

Calvin's heart sinks a little, but he doesn't give up. "What if we towed it to town? Maybe someone there can help?

Calvin feels a wave of disappointment washing over him at Mr. Farmer's words. "So, you might have to head into the city for parts? That's several days away from here."

"Several days?" Calvin replies, scratching his neck thoughtfully. "But you can't go tonight."

"You should rest and head out in the morning," Mr. Farmer says, his tone firm but kind.

"Yes," Mrs. Farmer chimes in, "It's getting dark soon, and the roads aren't safe at night. Plus, you've had quite an adventure today. You need your strength."

Calvin sighs, knowing they are right. The weight of the day's events is still heavy on his shoulders. "I appreciate it, really. I just… I feel like I need to be moving, you know? I want to get back home.

"Home will still be there in the morning," Mr. Farmer assures him. "You can't rush through this. Sometimes, the best way forward is to pause and gather your thoughts. We've got a spare room; you're welcome to stay the night."

"Why don't you stay the night?" Mrs. Farmer suggests warmly. "I can get the spare room already for you in no time. We'll make sure you're well-fed and ready to go in the morning."

Hayman smiles at Calvin, clearly pleased with the idea. "It'll give us time to plan your journey. Plus, I'd like to have a second helping of pie!" "Alright," Calvin says with a small smile, feeling grateful for their hospitality. "Thanks. I really appreciate it."

With that, the farmers show him to the spare room, a cozy space filled with soft linens and a small window overlooking the apple orchard. Calvin feels a wave of comfort as he sinks onto the bed, exhaustion catching up with him after the day's events.

As he lies there, he thinks about Montana and how worried his dog must be. But he also feels a flicker of hope—tomorrow, he will start his journey back home.

Chapter Eight
The Next Morning

Woken by the sound of Mr. Farmer's rooster crowing at sunrise, Calvin rolls over, greeted by the warm rays of the morning sun streaming through the window. A soft knock at the door announces Mr. Farmer's voice, "Breakfast is ready!"

"Be right down!" Calvin calls back, rubbing the sleep from his eyes. He swings his legs over the side of the bed, taking a moment to gather his thoughts about the strange events of the past day.

After a quick wash, he makes his way down the stairs, the delicious aroma of breakfast drawing him in. As he enters the dining room, he is met with a spread that makes his stomach growl: fluffy pancakes stacked high, crispy bacon, eggs, and hash browns, all accompanied by fresh milk and orange juice.

"Good morning!" Hayman greets him, already seated and enjoying a plateful.

"Did you sleep well, son?" Mrs. Farmer asks, a warm smile on her face.

Calvin smiles, feeling a warmth in his chest at Mrs. Farmer's kind words. As he prepares his plate, he loads it with pancakes, bacon, and a generous serving of hash browns, the delicious smells making his mouth water.

Sitting down, he takes a moment to enjoy the bustling atmosphere. Mr. Farmer shares stories about the crops and the weather, while Hayman chimes in with tales of the cornfield and his adventures as the watcher.

"Do you always get guests out here?" Calvin asks between bites.

"Not often," Mr. Farmer replies, pouring himself a cup of coffee. "Life in the country can be quiet, but we enjoy it. It's nice to have some excitement now and then."

Calvin nods, feeling grateful for their hospitality. "I really appreciate it. I was just trying to get dog food and ended up here," he chuckles.

"Sometimes the best adventures start with a simple trip to the store," Hayman says, grinning.

As they finish breakfast, Mrs. Farmer clears the table and brings out a fresh pot of coffee and juice, inviting them to linger a bit longer. Calvin feels content, savoring the moment. The warmth of the farmhouse and the kindness of the farmers make him forget, even if just for a while, the strange turn his life has taken.

After breakfast, Hayman leans back in his chair. "So, what's the plan for today?"

Calvin feeling a mix of excitement and curiosity, replies, "I really want to head to town, but I'd also love to explore a bit of Gold Valley.

Mrs. Farmer bustles around the kitchen, gathering items for a sack lunch. She fills it with homemade sandwiches, fresh fruit, and some of her famous apple pie, carefully wrapping everything in brown paper. "You boys are going to need some energy for your journey," she says with a warm smile.

Calvin watches as she adds a couple of cookies for good measure, her kindness evident in every detail. "Thank you so much, Mrs. Farmer. This is generous of you," he says, touched by her thoughtfulness.

Hayman chimes in, "You really know how to take care of us!" His straw arms wave in excitement.

"Your wagon will be safe here," Mr. Farmer assures Calvin, with a smile. "We've got plenty of room in the barn, and I'll keep an eye on it. You can find what you need in town."

Relieved, Calvin replies, "Thank you so much. I really appreciate all your help."

Mrs. Farmer chimes in, "And don't forget to take this!" She hands Calvin a sack filled with food for their journey. "It'll keep you fueled for your adventure."

Calvin takes the sack gratefully. "You're too kind. I can't thank you enough."

Mr. Farmer leans in, looking serious. "Just remember to stay on the yellow road. When you reach a fork in the path, there'll be a sign pointing you toward the city. It's hard to miss."

Calvin nods, taking mental notes. "Got it! Stay on the yellow road and look for the sign."

Hayman chimes in, "And keep an eye out for anything unusual. You never know what you might find along the way!"

Mrs. Farmer smiles warmly. "Just be careful. The land of Oz can be full of surprises."

Calvin feels a mix of excitement and apprehension as he imagines what lies ahead. "I will. Thanks again for everything. I'll make sure to be back soon."

Chapter Nine
The Journey

As they approach the fork in the road, Calvin, and Hayman exchange glances, both eager and uncertain. The sign stands at the split, but the wind has twisted it, making the direction to the city hard to decipher.

"Which way do you think we should go?" Calvin asks, squinting at the sign that seems to point in two different directions.

Hayman scratches his head, looking puzzled. "Well, not sure," he says, stepping closer to the sign. "But the wind had knocked the sign off the post." Calvin feels a flutter of unease. "What if we go the wrong way? We need to head off in the direction of the city.

"Let's trust our instincts," Hayman suggests. "We could take a moment to listen to the sounds around us. Sometimes the land tells you where to go."

Calvin nods, closing his eyes for a moment to focus. He listens intently, hearing the rustle of leaves and the distant chirping of birds. "I don't hear anything but the normal sound of nature," he says, opening his eyes with a hint of disappointment.

Hayman chuckles softly. "That's often how it starts. But sometimes, you just need to look a little closer or listen a little harder."

Let's go left!" Hayman replies, confidence returning to his voice. Calvin smiles, feeling encouraged by his friend's enthusiasm. "Left it is, then!"

With a shared determination, they choose the path that feels right and continue their journey, unaware of the misdirection that awaits them.

As they reach another fork in the road, Calvin stops to assess their options. To the left, the path appears well-trodden, with signs of recent activity. To the right, the trail is overgrown and winding, disappearing into the shadows of the trees.

Calvin turns to Hayman. "Which way do you think we should go?"

Hayman squints at the paths. "The left looks safer, but the right might hold some surprises. I've heard tales of hidden treasures and magical creatures in those woods."

"Treasure sounds nice," Calvin muses. "But we should prioritize getting to the city."

"Agreed," Hayman says, "But if we take the left path, we might miss something valuable."

Calvin ponders for a moment, then points to the left. "Let's stick to the safer route for now. We can always explore the right path later if we have time."

They set off down the left path, which is clear and easy to navigate. As they walk, they chat about their hopes of reaching the city and what they may find there. The air is crisp, and the forest gradually begins to open, revealing glimpses of the sky above.

After a while, Calvin notices something shiny on the ground just off the path. "Wait, what's that?" He walks over to investigate, kneeling to pick up a small, intricately designed compass.

Hayman's eyes widen. "That looks old! It might have belonged to someone who traveled these woods before us."

Calvin turns the compass over from one hand to the other, examining it closely. The needle spins wildly before finally settling, pointing steadfastly to the east. "It's definitely trying to tell us something," he remarks, furrowing his brow.

"This could be useful," he says, feeling a thrill of excitement. "Maybe it's guiding us toward something we need."

"Or it could lead us into more trouble," Hayman cautions, but there is a glint of curiosity in his eyes.

"Either way, let's keep it with us," Calvin decides. "It might come in handy."

With the compass in hand, they resume their journey, the forest surrounding them alive with possibilities.

Chapter Ten
Poppy Flowers

As they continue along the path, Calvin and Hayman soon find themselves approaching a stunning field of orange poppies. The vibrant flowers sway gently in the breeze, creating a mesmerizing sea of color stretching for miles.

"Wow," Calvin breathes, taking in the beauty. "It's like something out of a dream."

Hayman nods, a look of wonder on his face. "These poppies are special. They say they can make you feel at peace or even dreamier than usual. But be careful, some stories warn that you can fall asleep in a field like this and wake up somewhere else entirely."

Calvin chuckles nervously. "No sleeping for me! We have a mission."

Suddenly, Hayman pauses, sniffing the air. "Do you smell that? It's... different."

Calvin frowns, trying to identify the scent. "It's almost like something baking?"

Just then, they spot a small, rustic cottage nestled at the edge of the poppy field, smoke curling from the chimney. It looks inviting, with a thatched roof and colorful flower boxes.

"Should we check it out?" Calvin suggests, glancing at Hayman.

"Why not?" Hayman replies, his curiosity piqued. "Maybe we'll find someone who can help us on our journey."

As they approach the cottage, the sweet aroma grows stronger, making Calvin's stomach rumble. They knock on the door, and after a moment, it creaks open to reveal a cheerful woman with a warm smile.

"Welcome, travelers! Come in, come in! I've just baked some fresh pies!" she exclaims, her eyes twinkling.

Calvin and Hayman exchange excited glances before stepping inside, drawn in by the promise of warmth and delicious food. The interior is cozy, filled with the scent of baked goods and the sound of a crackling fire.

"Please, make yourselves at home!" the woman says, gesturing to a table laden with various pies and treats. "I'm Grandma Marigold. What brings you two to my poppy field?"

Calvin smiles, feeling the warmth of her hospitality. "We're on our way to the city, but we could use some help and maybe a little guidance."

"Ah, the city! It's a wonderful place, but it can be tricky to navigate. Sit, eat, and let me share some wisdom about your journey."

As they settle in, Calvin can't shake the feeling that they have stumbled upon something special. The adventure is becoming more unexpected with every step.

Calvin turns; his senses heightened. The cozy atmosphere of Grandma Marigold's cottage suddenly feels charged with anticipation. A soft rustling comes from the corner of the room, where a curtain flutters slightly as if disturbed by a breeze.

"Did you hear that?" Calvin whispers to Hayman, who is busy helping himself to a slice of pie.

Before Hayman can respond, a small creature pokes its head out from behind the curtain. It is a tiny, fluffy animal with big eyes and floppy ears, resembling a cross between a rabbit and a puppy.

"Hello there!" Grandma Marigold says, chuckling. "That's just Pippin. He's harmless—more curious than anything."

Calvin feels a wave of relief washes over him, but he is still intrigued. "What kind of creature is he?"

"Oh, Pippin is a Poppyskin," she explains, reaching down to pet the little creature. "They're known to be quite playful and are often found in fields of poppies. He loves to explore!"

Pippin hops closer, sniffing at Calvin's shoes with curiosity. He crouches down to get a better look. "You're adorable!" Calvin exclaims, reaching out a hand for Pippin to sniff.

As Pippin nuzzles his fingers, Grandma Marigold continues, "Now, tell me more about your journey. It sounds quite adventurous!"

Somewhat scared, Calvin looks at Grandma Marigold and says, "I really need to get to town to find parts to fix my wagon. I can't stay here too long."

Grandma Marigold pauses; her hands busy preparing tea for her guest. "I understand, dear. But with that storm brewing outside, it might not be safe for you to venture out just yet.

Calvin glances out the window, where dark clouds are rolling in and the wind is picking up. He feels a knot of anxiety tightening in his stomach. "I know, but I must get back to my dog and my mom. They're probably worried sick about me."

Hayman chimes in, "We'll head out as soon as it calms down. I don't want to be caught in the rain either. Maybe we can gather some supplies here to take with us?"

Grandma Marigold nods. "That's a good idea. I have plenty of food and a few tools that might help. But you'll need to wait a bit, dear. The weather can change quickly around here."

Calvin sighs, feeling torn. "I just feel so lost. Everything is so different here. I didn't even know this place existed until yesterday."

Pippin, sensing Calvin's unease, nuzzles closer, offering a small comfort. "You're not alone," Hayman says, placing a reassuring hand on Calvin's shoulder. "We'll figure this out together. Once the storm passes, we'll make our way to town. We just need to stick together."

Calvin nods, appreciating the support. "Okay, I'll try to be patient. I just hope the storm doesn't last too long."

Calvin tries to shake off the drowsiness creeping over him, but the warmth of the tea feels like a heavy blanket wrapping around him. He glances at Hayman, who is blissfully enjoying the delicious pies, completely oblivious to Calvin's struggle.

"Hey, Hayman," Calvin says, his voice slightly slurred. "I think there's something in this tea…"

But Hayman is too caught up in his feast to notice. Calvin's vision starts to blur, and he fights to stay alert. Panic surges through him as he realizes he might be falling under some sort of enchantment, like the little girl in the stories.

He looks around the cozy cottage, searching for a way to escape this drowsy feeling. "Pippin!" he calls softly, hoping the little dog can sense his distress.

The dog lifts its head, ears perked up, but it seems to sense that something is off, too. Calvin pushes himself to stand, but the room sways, and he stumbles slightly. "Hayman!" he tries again, louder this time. "I think we need to go — now!"

Finally, Hayman turns, concerned, replacing the carefree look on his face as he notices Calvin's pale complexion. "What's wrong?"

"I don't know, but I feel strange… I think tea might make me sleepy. We should leave before it gets worse!"

Grandma Marigold, hearing the urgency in their voices, steps closer. "Oh, dear! It's just a calming tea! I didn't mean to make you feel unwell."

Calvin shakes his head. "It's not just calming; it's like… it's trying to put me to sleep! We have to go!"

With a newfound determination, Hayman quickly finishes his pie and rushes to Calvin's side. "Let's get out of here, then! We can find our way to town and figure out the rest later."

Calvin nods, and together they hurry toward the door, Pippin at their heels. Just as they step outside, a gust of wind whips past them as if urging them forward. The storm clouds loom overhead, but Calvin feels a surge of clarity. They have to keep moving — no matter what.

Calvin shakes his head, trying to shake off the lingering drowsiness. "I think the tea was enchanted or something. It was like she wanted to put me to sleep and keep me here."

Hayman frowns: concern etched on his straw-stuffed face. "That's not good. You can't trust everyone you meet on the road, especially in a place like this."

Calvin nods, his heart racing a bit. "I guess I got a bit too comfortable. But we must stay alert. We can't let our guard down again."

As they continue along the yellow road, Calvin can't help but glance back at the cottage, now just a small dot in the distance. "What if she tries to follow us?" he wonders aloud.

"I don't think she can," Hayman replies, glancing over his shoulder as well. "Once you leave, it's hard to come back. But we should keep moving just in case."

They walk silently for a while, rustling leaves filling the air. The path is clear ahead, but Calvin feels a sense of unease lingering, like shadows lurking just out of sight.

"Do you think we'll make it to town?" Calvin asks, trying to refocus on their goal.

"Of course! Just stick to the road and keep your eyes peeled for any signs. We'll get there." Hayman's confidence is reassuring, and

Calvin takes a deep breath, determined to push through any obstacles.

Calvin glances over his shoulder, half-expecting to see the old lady or someone else lurking in the shadows. The trees loom taller and denser, their branches twisting together like gnarled fingers. "Hayman, do you feel that?" he whispers, trying to keep his voice steady.

Hayman pauses, tilting his head. "Feel what?"

"Like… we're being watched," Calvin replies, scanning the tree line. "I can't shake this feeling."

"Let's just keep moving," Hayman says, his voice firm. "If someone is following us, we can't let them catch up."

As they walk faster, Calvin's heart races. The rustling leaves seem to echo his anxiety. Every snap of a twig feels amplified, and shadows dance just out of sight. "What if it's someone from the old lady's place?" Calvin suggests, his imagination running wild.

"Then we'll be ready," Hayman replies, puffing out his chest. "We'll show them we're not afraid."

Just then, a soft thud echoes behind them, followed by a low growl. Calvin and Hayman stop in their tracks, eyes wide. "Did you hear that?" Calvin asks, his voice barely above a whisper.

Hayman nods, looking serious. "We should find a place to hide."

Chapter Eleven
The Wolf

Calvin's heart drops as he catches sight of the figure moving through the trees. The red eyes seem to glow with an eerie intensity, and he can feel Hayman tense beside him. "What is that?" Calvin whispers, trying to keep his voice steady.

"I don't know," Hayman replies, his voice trembling slightly. "But it doesn't look friendly."

The figure steps closer, revealing more of its shape—a hulking silhouette covered in dark fur, with long claws and a jagged snarl. The wolf, sensing the presence of the newcomer, lowers its head and growls, baring its teeth.

Calvin's mind races. "Should we run?" he whispers urgently.

Hayman shakes his head. "Not yet. We need to stay hidden and see what it does."

The creature moves cautiously, its eyes scanning the surroundings. Calvin feels the weight of its gaze as if it is searching for something—or someone. Suddenly, it lets out a low growl, almost as if it is communicating.

The wolf growls louder, stepping protectively in front of them. The dark figure seems to take a step back, confused. Calvin's pulse quickens; he can feel the tension crackling in the air.

"What if it's looking for us?" he whispers, his heart racing. "What if it's part of that old lady's magic?"

Just then, the figure turns its head toward their hiding spot, locking eyes with Calvin. He feels a chill run down his spine as the creature's gaze bears into him as if it can see right through the trees.

"Now would be a good time to move," Hayman urges, his voice a low whisper.

Calvin nods, slowly inching backward, but before they make a break for it, the dark figure lunges forward towards them.

Calvin freezes mid-swing, the branch hovering in the air. The wolf's voice is deep and rumbling, but it holds an unexpected hint of curiosity rather than aggression.

"Wait," Calvin says, lowering the branch slightly. "You can talk?"

"Of course, I can talk," the wolf replies, standing tall and looking down at them with piercing eyes. "Now, who are you two, and what brings you into my territory?"

Hayman steps forward, still wary but intrigued. "We're just travelers trying to reach the city. We got a bit lost along the way."

The wolf's expression softens a fraction. "Lost, you say? Many who wander through these woods become trapped in their fears or the enchantments of others. Tell me, what spell has led you here?"

Calvin glances at Hayman, unsure whether to share their encounter with the old lady. "We… we met an old woman who offered us tea. It made me feel strange."

The wolf nods knowingly. "Ah, yes. The Enchantress of the Woods. She often lures wanderers with promises of hospitality but ensnares them with her magic. You were wise to escape her."

Calvin reaches for a branch that he holds firmly, his knuckles white as he raises it like a baseball bat. "We mean no harm!" he declares, his voice steady despite the fear churning in his stomach.

The wolf pauses, its red eyes narrowing as it studies Calvin. "Is that so?" it replies, tilting its head slightly. "Then lower your weapon, and let's talk. I'm not here to fight unless provoked."

Calvin hesitates, his grip tightening on the branch. "How do I know you won't attack us?"

The wolf sighs, a deep rumbling sound that echoes through the trees. "I have no interest in harming travelers unless they give me a reason to. Now, if you truly seek the city, I can help you, but first, I need to know you're honest."

Reluctantly, Calvin lowers the branch but keeps it within reach. "We just want to get to the city. We need parts to fix my car — uh, I mean my wagon. I promise we're not looking for trouble."

Hayman nods in agreement, stepping closer to Calvin. "We're just two friends trying to find our way home. The wolf's instincts are on high alert, its body taut with tension as it crouches low, eyes locked on the stranger, Calvin. The words from Calvin's lips seem to hold no weight in the wolf's world, where trust is earned, not spoken into existence. Every movement, every sound, scrutinized by the animal's sharp senses, and Calvin's presence only bred suspicion.

Slowly, the wolf creeps down, its body inching lower, muscles coiling like a spring. It can feel the ground beneath its paws, each step measured and deliberate. There is no need for a warning, no growl or barring of teeth. The animal's actions speak louder than any vocal threat — it prepares for something far more decisive.

Then, without hesitation, the wolf pounces.

In a fluid, almost predatory motion, it leaps from its hiding spot, its powerful legs propelling it through the air, eyes fixed on its target. The jump is swift and silent, a blur of fur and raw strength. Calvin has no time to react before the wolf is on him, its instincts having already decided the stranger is a threat.

In those fleeting moments, everything else in the world fades—the only reality is the wolf's jump and Calvin's uncertain fate.

Calvin hits the ground with a heavy thud, the air knocked out of him as the wolf's massive form descends in a blur of fur and teeth. Before he can fully comprehend what is happening, the weight of the creature is on top of him, pressing him into the cold, unforgiving earth. The force of the impact leaves him stunned, breathless, and vulnerable.

The wolf's body is heavy, its muscles and sinew pressing down, making it almost impossible to move. Calvin can feel the heat radiating from the animal, the powerful movement of its chest with each breath it takes. The wild scent of fur and earth fills the air as the wolf's claws dig into the ground near him, poised to strike.

The animal's face hovers dangerously close, its amber eyes glowing unsettlingly. It snarls low, a warning growl reverberating through Calvin's chest. Every instinct in his body screams to fight, to escape, but the weight of the wolf, combined with the fear of its next move, leaves him paralyzed.

His heart races in his chest, the overwhelming pressure of the moment closing in on him. Calvin knows he has only moments before the wolf makes its next move—he has to act, or the consequences will be dire.

"Get off me!" Calvin shouts, struggling to push the creature away. The wolf's red eyes glint with primal hunger; its teeth bare in a snarl.

From behind the tree, Hayman peers out, his heart racing. "Calvin!" he yells, unsure whether to help or stay hidden. "What can I do?"

"Distract it!" Calvin shouts, pushing against the wolf's chest with all his might. The creature shifts slightly, its focus torn between Calvin and the sound of Hayman's voice.

In a moment of desperation, Hayman grabs a nearby rock and hurls it at the wolf. The rock misses, but the noise startles the creature enough to make it glance back. "Over here, you big mutt!" Hayman yells, trying to draw the wolf's attention.

Chapter Twelve
The Lion

Calvin's heart pounds in his chest, each beat hammering against his ribs as the weight of the wolf presses down on him, pinning him to the ground. The air is tense, the wolf's growl vibrating through the earth beneath him. Its amber eyes locked onto Calvin with an unnerving focus, its claws digging into the soil beside him. Calvin's breath comes in shallow gasps, his body freezes beneath the relentless pressure of the beast.

Just as he thought he might lose control; a flicker of movement catches his eye. Through the blur of his panicked vision, Calvin sees a shadow shift — something — or someone — peeking around the tree at the edge of the clearing. His pulse spikes. Who is that? Another threat? Or is it a chance at salvation?

His mind races, trying to process the figure, but the wolf's weight keeps him from moving, from calling out. The figure remains still, just beyond the wolf's line of sight, watching the scene unfold with a quiet intensity. Calvin can barely make out any details — just the faintest outline.

The larger creature — a massive, muscular beast with dark fur — suddenly leaps at the wolf, catching it off guard. The two animals collide with a ferocious growl, rolling onto the ground in a tangle of fur and teeth.

"What is that?" Hayman whispers, eyes wide with a mix of fear and awe.

"I have no idea," Calvin replies, as he gets up and makes a dash toward the location where Hayman is hiding. Calvin gripping the tree tightly. "But I hope it knows what it's doing!"

The larger creature pins the wolf down, its size and strength overwhelming. The wolf snarls, struggling beneath its weight, but the newcomer is relentless. With a swift, powerful bite, it clamps down on the wolf's neck, causing the wolf to yelp in pain.

Calvin and Hayman exchange glances, unsure whether to stay hidden or make a run for it while the two creatures fight for control. "Should we go?" Hayman asks, his voice trembling.

"Maybe we should wait a moment," Calvin suggests, still watching the fight unfold. "If that thing can take down the wolf, we might have a chance to escape."

Just then, the wolf lets out a final howl, trying to break free, but the larger creature holds its ground. With one last effort, the wolf twists, and bolts into the trees, retreating from the fight.

The larger creature stands tall, panting heavily, before turning to face Calvin and Hayman. Its eyes, fierce but strangely intelligent, lock onto theirs. Calvin feels a surge of both fear and curiosity.

"Are we safe?" he whispers to Hayman.

Calvin's heart races as the imposing figure of the lion approaches. Its golden mane glints in the dappled sunlight filtering through the trees, and its eyes are sharp and watchful.

"I'm Titan, protector of these woods," the lion says, standing before Calvin and Hayman, ready to defend those that are in need for help.

The lion pauses, sizing up the situation. "And what do you need protection from?" he asks, his voice a deep growl that resonates through the clearing.

"We're just trying to get to the city," Calvin replies, trying to sound more confident than he feels. "We got lost on the yellow road and ran into some trouble."

The lion narrows his eyes. "Trouble? In these woods, it's best to keep your wits about you. What kind of trouble?"

"A wolf attacked us," Hayman chimes in, still shaken from the encounter. "But you came along and helped us."

The lion studied them, then nods slowly. That wolf has been a nuisance lately."

Calvin glances at the lion, who looks proud but also concerned. "We appreciate your help," Calvin continues. "We were told to follow the yellow road to the city, but it seems we've strayed off track."

The lion's expression softens slightly. "The yellow road can be tricky. It changes and misleads. But I can guide you to the fork where you'll find the correct path."

"Thank you," Calvin says, relief washing over him. "That would be great."

"Very well," the lion says, turning gracefully. "Follow me. Stay close, and don't stray."

As they walk, Calvin feels a strange sense of camaraderie with the lion. Despite the fear and uncertainty, there is a strange magic to this place, a sense of adventure that pushes him forward. He glances at Hayman, who seems to share his resolve.

"What's your name, boy?" the lion asks, glancing back at Calvin.

"I'm Calvin," he replies. "And this is Hayman."

"Calvin and Hayman," the lion muses. "Names that carry strength. Let's see if that strength can guide you home." Haymen asks, the lion what's your name? The lion replies I am Titan.

With that, the trio set off deeper into the woods, ready to face whatever lies ahead.

Traveling for hours in the woods the sun seems to set slowly in the distance. Calvin asks Titan if they can find a place to rest for the night. "We both have been traveling for several hours now and we are getting tired." Titan, the lion, pauses and looks around. The sun dips lower in the sky, casting long shadows through the trees. "You're right, Calvin," he says, his deep voice resonating in the quiet. "It's wise to rest before nightfall. The woods can become treacherous in the dark."

"I know a safe spot not far from here," he says. "There's a clearing with some thick brush. It'll provide good shelter."

"Lead the way," Calvin replies, feeling grateful for their companionship. As they follow Titan, he can't shake the feeling of unease that often creeps in at night.

Chapter Thirteen
Abandoned House

As they approach the clearing, Calvin's eyes are drawn to the old, abandoned house partially obscured by thick bushes. The once-white paint is now peeling, and the roof sags under the weight of years. Vines snake their way up the walls, and the windows are mostly shattered, giving the place a hauntingly eerie vibe.

"What do you think happened here?" Calvin asks, stepping closer, his curiosity piqued.

Titan, who has been observing the surroundings, replies, "This place has been empty for ages. People say it was a home long ago, but stories go that it was left behind after something strange happened."

"Some say the family who lived here vanished without a trace," Titan says, his voice low. "Others claim it's haunted by their spirits. But it could just be a story to scare children."

Calvin feels a shiver run down his spine. "Should we check it out?"

Titan ponders for a moment. "We need to rest, but it could hold something useful. Just remember, we should be cautious."

The three of them make their way toward the house, the sounds of the forest fading behind them. As they approach, the door swings slightly in the wind, creaking ominously. Calvin hesitates but takes a deep breath and steps inside.

The interior is dim, with dust motes dancing in the shafts of light filtering through the broken windows. Old furniture lies strewn about, covered in layers of dust. A musty smell fills the air, mixed with a hint of something sweet and rotten.

"Wow, this place feels like it's frozen in time," Calvin remarks, glancing at a cobweb-covered chair.

Hayman moves cautiously, his eyes darting around. "Let's not touch anything. We don't know what could be lurking here."

Calvin nods, but his curiosity compels him to explore further. As he steps into what appears to be the main room, he notices an ornate mirror hanging crookedly on the wall. The glass is murky, but it seems to shimmer with an otherworldly light.

"Hey, check this out!" he calls to the others, moving closer to the mirror.

Titan approaches, a cautious look on his face. "Careful, Calvin. Mirrors can sometimes reflect more than just our appearances."

As Calvin reaches out to touch the mirror's surface, he feels a strange pulse emanating from it. The reflection wavers, and for a moment, he thinks he sees a flicker of movement behind him.

"Did you see that?" Calvin exclaims, turning to look at Titan and Hayman.

"What?" Hayman asks, stepping closer, eyes wide.

"I thought I saw something in the reflection," Calvin says, feeling a mix of excitement and dread. "Like a shadow moving behind me."

Titan frowns, glancing at the mirror. "We should be on our guard. This place feels like it holds secrets — secrets we might not be ready to uncover."

Calvin squints at the interior of the house, trying to shake off a strange sense of familiarity. The faded wallpaper, the layout, even the peculiar smell — something tugs at the edges of his memory. "I've seen this house before," he murmurs, almost to himself.

"Seen it where?" Hayman asks, tilting his head in curiosity.

"I'm not sure. Maybe in a dream or something," Calvin replies, stepping further into the room. The mirror still shimmers, and he finds himself drawn to it again as if it holds the key to his memories.

Titan watches him closely. "Dreams can sometimes reveal more than we think. Maybe you have a connection to this place."

Calvin nods, his heart racing. He reaches out to touch the mirror once more, feeling the cool glass beneath his fingers. "What if this house has something to do with why I ended up in Gold Valley Oz?"

Hayman moves closer, his eyes narrowing. "What do you mean?"

"I don't know. Maybe something happened here that brought me to this land," Calvin speculates. "Maybe it's linked to the old stories."

Titan steps beside him, a thoughtful expression on his face. "We should dig deeper. If this place has a connection to you, it might also hold answers."

Calvin feels a surge of determination. "Let's explore it, then. If there's anything here that can help us—anything that can get me back home—we need to find it."

As they begin to search the house, moving from room to room, Calvin can't shake the feeling that he is retracing steps he has taken before, uncovering layers of a past he doesn't fully understand. The air feels thick with possibility, and he can't help but wonder what secrets lie hidden within these walls.

Titan's eyes sparkle with nostalgia as he shares his memory. "My parents brought me here when I was just a little cub. They said this house was once a gathering place for creatures from all over Oz. It was filled with laughter and stories."

Titan's expression darkens slightly. "After the great storm, everything changed. The house fell into disrepair, and the gatherings stopped. It became a place of whispers and legends—a place people avoided."

Hayman steps closer, brushing some dust off an old chair. "So, you think there might still be something valuable here? Something that can help Calvin?"

Titan nods. "It's possible. This house may hold remnants of its past—objects, stories, even magic. If it connects to both of you, we should uncover what we can."

As the flames crackle to life, warmth spreads through the room, casting flickering shadows on the walls. Titan settles next to Hayman, creating a protective barrier as they all gather close to the fire.

Calvin takes a deep breath, feeling a sense of comfort in their little gathering. "I know this place feels eerie, but it's actually kind of cozy," he says, glancing at the worn furniture and the old paintings that still adorn the walls.

Hayman nods, his earlier fear fading. "Yeah, it's not so bad with the fire. Just feels like stories are waiting to be told here."

Titan leans back, his golden fur catching the firelight. "This house has seen many adventures.

Titan's voice takes on a hushed, reverent tone as he shares the story. "My father used to tell me about this house. He said it fell from the sky and landed right on the Wicked Witch of the North, ending her reign of terror. The townsfolk were both grateful and fearful, for they believed the house carried powerful magic.

Calvin leans in, captivated. "So, this place is… famous?"

Hayman nods, eyes wide. "Famous and feared. Some say it still holds remnants of that witch's magic. That's why I was always warned to stay away."

Titan continues, "After the witch's defeat, the house was left empty, a relic of the past. Some believe it's haunted, while others think it's a sanctuary for lost souls. My parents brought me here once, hoping to show me the strength of courage and friendship. They believed that even in darkness, light could be found."

Calvin shivers slightly. "So, is it true? Do you think the witch's spirit lingers here?"

Titan shrugs, a thoughtful expression on his face. "I don't know. But I do believe places hold memories, and this house has seen a lot. Maybe it's not about fear but rather understanding the stories it holds."

Hayman, still cuddled close to Titan, looks around nervously. "Well, as long as the fire keeps burning, I'm okay with whatever spirits might be here."

Calvin chuckles, trying to lighten the mood. "If any spirits show up, we can just invite them to join our campfire!"

Chapter Fourteen
The Next Day

Hayman blinks awake, his eyes darting around the dimly lit room. The sound of chewing is unmistakable and seems to be coming from just beyond the shadows.

"Titan?" he whispers, nudging the lion beside him. "Do you hear that?"

Titan stirs, his ears twitching at the noise. "Yeah, I do. Stay quiet."

As he leans up, he is being overtaken by the black rats that are gnawing on his legs. Hayman lets out a scream at the same time kicking the black rats off him. Calvin jolts upright, panic flooding his senses as he feels the sharp bites of the black rats gnawing at his legs. Hayman's scream echoes through the room, a mix of terror and surprise.

"Get them off! Get them off!" Hayman yells, kicking wildly. The rats scurry away, their tiny bodies darting back into the shadows, but not before leaving a few nips on Calvin's shins.

"Whoa! What's happening?" Titan growls, springing to his feet, his mane bristling in alarm.

"Rats! There were rats!" Hayman gasps, still trying to shake off the remnants of his fright. "I didn't see them until it was too late!"

Calvin winces as he inspects his legs, relieved to find only minor scratches. "I think they were just as surprised as we were," he says, trying to calm the situation. "This place must be crawling with them."

As Hayman is all mended. He tells them, "OK, we should leave and get back on the road. We still have a long journey ahead." As they all head towards the door that is when Calvin sees a picture of a lady holding a basket of what appears to be muffins-like bread. Calvin pauses, captivated by the picture. The woman in the frame has a kind smile, her apron dusted with flour, and she holds a basket filled with what looks like golden-brown muffins. "Hey, check this out!" he calls to Hayman and Titan.

"What is it?" Hayman asks, peering over Calvin's shoulder.

"Look at her. She looks like she might've been a baker or something," Calvin says, brushing dust off the glass. "I wonder if those muffins were any good."

Titan steps closer, examining the picture. "That could be a clue. If she lived here, she might have left something behind."

Calvin's eyes sparkle with curiosity. "Maybe there are some hidden treats in the kitchen!"

"Or more rats," Hayman mutters, still wary after their recent encounter. Hayman urges them, "We should go now before anything else happens. I don't want to stick around here any longer than we must."

Calvin nods, feeling the urgency in Hayman's voice. "You're right. Let's make sure we're out of this old place before more surprises come our way."

Titan takes a last look around the kitchen, ensuring they haven't missed anything useful. "Alright, let's head out. Stick together and remember to keep an eye out for any more… creatures."

As they step back into the living room, the sunlight is already filtering through the dusty windows, illuminating the path to the door. They make their way outside, feeling the fresh air wash over them.

"Which way do we go?" Calvin asks, glancing at the fork in the road they've encountered before.

Titan points down the path that leads into the trees. "We should stick to the road we came from. It should lead us back to the yellow road and hopefully toward the city."

"Let's go then," Hayman says, determination in his voice.

As they walk, the muffled sounds of the forest surround them, a mix of rustling leaves and distant animal calls. With each step, they feel a renewed sense of purpose, ready to face whatever challenges lie ahead.

Chapter Fifteen
Old Friend Tinman

After an hour or so of walking, Titan squints into the distance and points. "Hey, do you see that?"

Calvin and Hayman follow his gaze and spot a flickering light through the trees. "It looks like a campfire," Calvin says, his curiosity piqued. "Should we check it out?"

Titan nods. "It could be travelers, or it might be someone who can help us. But we should approach it carefully. We don't know who or what it is."

They move cautiously, making their way through the underbrush until they reach the edge of a small clearing.

As Titan steps closer to the fire, his eyes widen in recognition. "Wait a minute," he exclaims, "Is that you, Tinman?"

The figure sitting by the fire turns, and a broad smile spreads across his metallic face. "Titan! It's been ages!" He stands up, his joints creaking slightly, and embraces Titan with a warmth that seems almost surprising for someone made of tin.

Calvin and Hayman exchange curious glances. "You know him?" Calvin asks.

Titan nods enthusiastically. "We grew up together in these woods. The Tinman has quite the story—he's one of the bravest around!"

The Tinman chuckles, his voice a soft metallic chime. "I've had my share of adventures, that's for sure. But what brings you all here?"

"I am heading to the city with friends to see if someone could assist my friend with wagon parts so he can go home."

The Tinman nods, understanding the urgency in Calvin's voice. "Ah, I see. It sounds like quite the quest you're on! The journey to the city can be tricky, but with your friends by your side, you'll be fine."

Hayman chimes in, "We've heard a lot about the city. What's it like?"

"The Emerald City is a sight to behold," the Tinman replies, his eyes gleaming with nostalgia. "Tall towers made of shimmering green glass, bustling streets filled with all kinds of creatures, and the Wizard himself—who's a bit of a mystery but has a good heart."

Calvin leans forward, intrigued. "And you really think he can help us?"

As they settle in, the warmth of the fire wraps around them, and the sound of laughter fills the air. For the first time in a while, Calvin feels a sense of hope. Maybe, just maybe, they can find a way back home, after all.

Titan asks Tinman to join them on their trip. "It would be nice to talk about the old times with these youngsters."

Tinman's face lights up with a wide smile. "I would be honored! It's been too long since I've had an adventure, and I'd love to share some stories with you all."

Titan nods approvingly. "Great! The more, the merrier. Plus, we could use your knowledge of the area. It's easy to get lost in these woods."

As they make plans for the journey ahead, the Tinman started recounting tales of his past—stories of encounters with the Scarecrow, the Cowardly Lion, and even some misadventures with wicked witches. Laughter and camaraderie filled the air, providing a welcome distraction from the uncertainties that lay ahead.

Calvin felt a sense of belonging as he listened, grateful for the unexpected friendships forming around him. With the Tinman joining their group, the journey to the city seemed a little less daunting. They would face whatever challenges came their way together.

So, then Calvin asks the Tinman is the stories true about a little girl that killed a wicked witch back in the days? The farmer told us a story about how this city was filled with darkness.

The Tinman nodded, his expression growing serious. "Yes, the stories are true. That little girl, Dorothy, arrived in Oz quite unexpectedly. She had a way of bringing light to the darkest of places."

He paused, recalling the tales of old. "When she landed here, she accidentally crushed the Wicked Witch of the North with her house. That act freed the Munchkins from her tyranny, but it also drew the attention of the Wicked Witch of the West, who sought revenge."

Calvin leaned in, intrigued. "What happened then?"

"The Wicked Witch of the West sent her minions after Dorothy and her friends, but with the help of the Scarecrow, the Cowardly Lion, and my third-generation grandfather, they were able to confront her. In the end, it was Dorothy's courage and cleverness that defeated her. She threw water on the witch, and you know what happened next—she melted away!" The Tinman's voice held a mixture of nostalgia and pride.

"So, this place really has seen its share of darkness," Calvin mused. "And now it seems like it's up to us to keep that light shining."

Titan nodded, adding, "We all have a part to play in keeping Oz safe. It's a big responsibility, but together, we can face any challenge."

With renewed determination, the group continued down the path, ready to face whatever awaited them in the city.

Calvin then replies, why is there still the feeling of darkness that hangs on to this place still?

The Tinman sighed, his metal frame creaking slightly. "Even after the witch's defeat, darkness can linger in the hearts of those who have suffered. Fear, resentment, and doubt can take root in a community, especially after years of oppression. Not everyone has found their way back to the light."

Titan added, "There are still remnants of the witch's influence. Some creatures have grown bitter and distrustful, and there are tales of hidden dangers in the woods. It takes time and effort to heal."

Calvin frowned, absorbing this. "So, it's not just about defeating a villain; it's about mending a community?"

"Exactly," the Tinman replied. "Every act of kindness, every brave decision can help dispel the shadows. It's a slow process, but every little bit counts."

Hayman chimed in, "And with friends like us, we can support each other in this journey. Together, we can remind everyone that hope exists, even in the darkest of times."

Calvin nodded, feeling a sense of purpose building within him. "Then let's do our part. We may just be travelers, but maybe we can help light the way."

With that, the group pressed onward, determined to bring their own light into the world around them.

Chapter Sixteen
Munchkin

As the sun dips below the horizon, casting a golden hue over the forest, the four find themselves standing at the edge of the clearing where the Munchkins have once flourished. The air is thick with memories, and the haunting sounds of nature enveloped. It has been a long journey; one filled with whispers of an ancient species on the brink of extinction.

The Munchkins, small and vibrant creatures resembling a cross between mushrooms and delicate faeries, had thrived in these woods for centuries. Their luminescent caps had illuminated the forest at night, and their laughter had echoed through the trees. But now, they are nearly gone, victims of a changing world and encroaching in darkness.

Titan heart races as he recalls the tales his father told him, stories of their magic and the bond they shared with the land. He can feel the weight of his ancestors' hopes resting on his shoulders. The elders had entrusted him with a vital mission: to find the last Munchkins and restore their home.

As they step deeper into the clearing, Hayman notices a soft glow emanating from a thicket of moss and wildflowers. He approaches cautiously, his breath hitching his throat. Could it be? As Hayman parts the branches, a gasp escapes his lips.

There, nestled among the ferns, are the last three Munchkins, their caps shimmering like stars. They are small and delicate, their eyes wide with a mix of fear and curiosity. Hayman kneels, his heart aching at their fragility.

"Please, don't be afraid," he whispers, his voice gentle. "I'm here to help."

The Munchkins exchange glances, their tiny forms trembling. One steps forward, its cap flickering like a candle. "Help us?" it asks, its voice barely above a whisper.

"Yes," Hayman replies, feeling a surge of determination. "The forest is losing its magic, and without you, it will fade away. I want to bring you back to the Heartwood, where you can flourish once more."

The Munchkins huddle together, their light flickering in unison. "The Heartwood…" the brave one murmurs. "But it is guarded by shadows. They seek to extinguish our light."

"I know," Hayman says, standing tall. "But my friends and I are on our way to the city and maybe there we can find a way to vanish the darkness that plagued this area for years."

With a collective breath, the Munchkins nod. Their glow intensifies, illuminating the surrounding darkness. Hayman feels a warmth enveloping him as he reaches out, allowing their light to merge with him. At that moment, he understands their magic is intertwined with his spirit.

Hayman then turns back to the group to show them the last remaining Munchkins that he found hiding in the flowers. Calvin is amazed at how tiny they are and introduces himself to the small, tiny creatures.

Following him, the Titan, the lion introduces himself as does the Tinman. Together, they set off toward the city, each step resonating with hope and purpose. The path is fraught with danger, shadows lurking at the edges of the trees. But the team remain steadfast, their resolve unwavering in the face of uncertainty. Each member has their strengths and their reasons for fighting.

As they press onward, the canopy above thickens, casting long shadows across the forest floor. The air feels electric, charged with the remnants of their recent battle and the promise of the unknown ahead. Titan leads the way, his senses heightened. "Keep your eyes peeled," he says, glancing back at the group. "The shadows won't take defeat lightly."

Calvin nods, feeling the strength of their unity. They are a formidable team, each bringing their skills to the table. Tinman recalls the tales of the Heartwood—a sacred place where magic thrived, and balance reigned. If they can reach it, they may be able to restore what has been lost.

As they navigate the winding paths, the trees begin to shift, their trunks twisting and turning in ways that feel almost alive. The ground is covered in vibrant moss, softening their footsteps.

Chapter Seventeen
The Fawn

Suddenly, a rustle breaks the stillness. Titan holds up a paw, signaling for silence. The group freezes, their senses heightened. From the underbrush, a creature emerges a small, timid fawn, its eyes wide with fear.

"It's just a deer," Calvin whispers, relaxing slightly.

Both Titan and Tinman know no such creature as a deer has ever existed in Gold Valley. The land is steeped in legend and lore, populated by mythical beings and strange entities, but a simple deer is a foreign concept. As they stand at the edge of the forest, their mechanical minds struggle to understand the sight before them.

"What manner of creature is this?" Titan muses, his voice rumbling like distant thunder. His metallic form gleams in the fading light, a sentinel against the encroaching shadows.

"It seems harmless," Tinman replies, his eyes flickering with curiosity. "But what is it doing here? Could it be a sign?"

The appearance of the fawn, delicate and trembling, feels like an omen. It is clear the forest is undergoing changes, but what does this mean for their mission?

Just then, the fawn turns, its eyes wide locking onto theirs. It steps back, wary but unafraid. "You're not like the others," it says, its voice soft and melodic, sending shivers down their spines.

Titan and Tinman exchange bewildered glances. "Did you hear that?" Titan asks.

Calvin shrugs, a grin creeping onto his face. "Well, I was shocked when a tree spoke to me as well! And let's not forget the scarecrow, and both you and Titan. It seems anything is possible in this place."

Titan chuckles, the sound rumbling like distant thunder. "In Gold Valley, the lines between the ordinary and the extraordinary often blur. Perhaps this fawn is just another example of the magic that permeates this land."

The fawn tilts its head, sensing the curiosity of the group. "You seek the Heartwood," it says, taking a tentative step closer. "But the darkness is rising. You must hurry, or it will consume everything."

"Darkness?" Titan echoes, concern etching lines into his face. "What darkness?"

"The shadows that once slept are awakening," the fawn warns. "They crave the light of the Munchkin, and without help, they will destroy the magic of Gold Valley."

Tinman straightens, a new resolve igniting within him. "We must gather our allies and protect the Munchkin. They are the key to restoring balance."

"Yes," Titan agrees, his voice steady. "But we cannot act alone. We will need the strength of the forest and its magic."

The fawn nods, its expression earnest. "Follow me. I will take you to Heartwood. But be vigilant; the shadows will not let you pass easily."

As they follow the fawn deeper into the woods, Titan and Tinman feel the weight of their mission. They have met many challenges before, but this one feels different. The stakes are higher, the forces at play are more powerful.

Calvin steps forward, his eyes gleaming with urgency. "Wait!" he calls out, bringing the group to a halt.

Calvin nods, understanding the confusion. "Yes, we are heading to the city — that's been our plan all along. But with everything that's happened in the forest, I felt it was important to emphasize how crucial it is for us to seek help there, especially for me to find a way back home."

The fawn's voice trembles with urgency. "It's important to move quickly! If we linger here, the darkness will find us, and it will destroy the last remaining Munchkins."

Calvin feels a chill at the fawn's words. "We can't let that happen. We need to protect them at all costs."

Titan nods; his expression serious. "We're already behind. The longer we wait, the more vulnerable Munchkin becomes.

"I need to go to the city," Calvin says, urgency rising in his voice. "I have my dog and my mom both worrying about me now. I've been gone for way too long. I understand the mission to save the tiny creatures, but I need saving too."

The fawn pauses, its ears perked up in concern. "Your loved ones are important, Calvin. We will find a way to help them, but you must understand that the shadows threaten everyone here. If we don't act, there may not be a home to return to."

"Then let's go," Tinman urges, glancing around as shadows flickered at the edges of the clearing. "We can't waste another moment."

Calvin nods: his expression conflicted. "I get that, but I can't keep fighting something I can't see. It's hard to feel brave when the threat is lurking in the shadows."

The fawn's gaze softens. "I understand. The shadows are cunning, and their darkness can be overwhelming. But remember courage isn't the absence of fear; it's the decision to move forward despite it."

Titan steps closer, his presence steadying. "You're not alone in this fight. We're all in it together, and together we'll shine a light on what we face. The shadows may hide, but they can't withstand our unity."

With the fawn leading the way, they quicken their pace. The path narrows, winding through dense underbrush and towering trees, but the urgency of the moment propels them forward. The sounds of the forest fade into the background, replaced by the rhythmic pounding of their hearts.

As they move, Calvin can't shake the image of the vulnerable Munchkins from his mind. "Do you think they're safe for now?" he asks, glancing at the fawn.

"They're hidden," the fawn replies, glancing back with worry. "But the shadows are relentless. If they sense any weakness, they will strike."

As the six of them make their way through the forest, Titan, the lion suddenly freezes in his tracks. The others halt as well, sensing the shift in his demeanor.

"There!" Titan points with a massive paw, his golden eyes wide with awe. "In the distance… it's Heartwood!"

The fawn's eyes sparkle with excitement. "The Heartwood! It's a sacred place, where magic flows strongest. If we can reach it, we may find guidance and strength."

Yet, something seems odd as they look straight ahead at Heartwood. The vibrant glow that had initially filled them with hope now flickers uncertainly, casting eerie shadows among the ancient trees. The air feels charged, but there is an underlying tension that makes Calvin's skin crawl.

Chapter Eighteen
Heartwood

"Something is watching us," Tinman murmurs, his metal frame tense. "We should proceed carefully."

"Foolish travelers," it hisses, the voice echoing around them. "You dare to approach the Heartwood while the darkness awakens? You will regret it!"

Calvin feels a rush of adrenaline. "We're here to protect the Heartwood and the Munchkins! We won't let you harm them!"

The figure laughs, a chilling sound that sends shivers down his spine. "Protect? You are but a small band of misfits. The Heartwood's magic is fading, and soon, it will belong to the shadows."

The fawn steps forward, its voice trembling but defiant. "We won't let that happen! We are as stronger than you think!"

As tension fills the air, Calvin feels the weight of their mission pressing down on him. This is the moment they have been preparing for. "We need to stand together!" he shouts. "We can't let fear take hold!"

With that, they form a circle, ready to confront the darkness threatening Heartwood. The figure sneers, shadows swirling around it like a cloak, but the glow of the Heartwood pulses stronger in response to their unity.

Titan steps forward, a fierce protector. "You will not take this place! We will fight for the light!"

As the shadows close in, the group braces themselves, ready to defend not just Heartwood, but their hopes for the future. The battle for Gold Valley — and for Calvin's way home — is about to begin.

"Fools!" the figure hisses, its voice echoing through the darkness. "You think you can protect the Heartwood? It belongs to the shadows now!"

Calvin clenches his fists, determination surging through him. "We won't let you take it! This forest is alive, and we will fight for it!"

The fawn stands at his side, its small form radiating an aura of light. "Together, we can push back the darkness!"

As the figure lunges, Titan charges forward, his powerful roar cutting through the air. "Stand strong!" he bellows, rallying his friends. The ground trembles as he meets the shadows head-on, his form a beacon of strength.

Tinman raises his axe, prepared to strike. "We need to illuminate the shadows! We have to show them the power of light!"

At that point, Hayman looks down into his pocket, where he has kept the Munchkins safe. A flicker of inspiration crosses his mind. "Maybe… just maybe, if I bring them out, they can shine their light against the dark shadow," he thinks.

"Do you think it would work?" he asks, glancing at his companions, who are still catching their breath from the confrontation. "The Munchkins have a unique magic of their own. If they could join our light, perhaps we could push back the darkness even further."

The fawn's eyes widen with excitement. "Yes! The Munchkins are filled with the essence of the forest. Their light could amplify our strength!"

Calvin nods, his heart racing. "We need all the light we can get. If we can harness the Munchkins' magic, it could make a real difference."

With determination, Hayman carefully reaches into his pocket and pulls out one of the small Munchkin. Its gentle glow illuminates his face, casting soft light on the shadows surrounding them. "Come on, little one," he says softly, "We need your help."

As the Munchkin appears, its light brightens, and soon others follow, filling the space around them with a warm, radiant glow. The darkness seems to hiss and recoil at the sight.

The shadowy figure, now lurking at the edges of their vision, snarls in frustration. "You think those tiny lights can defeat me?" it sneers, but even it seems hesitant, the confidence wavering.

Hayman holds the Munchkin high, feeling its energy pulsate in his hand. "Together, we can illuminate the darkness!"

As he reaches into his pocket he takes out the other Munchkins join the first, their collective glow intensifies, creating a brilliant sphere of light that surrounds the group. The shadows that have once loomed over them begin to retreat, flickering like candle flames in a strong wind.

"Feel the power of the forest!" the fawn shouts, its voice rising above the chaos. "Together, we are stronger!"

With their newfound strength, the light from the Munchkins surges forward, driving the shadows back. The dark figure hisses, its form destabilizing as the brilliance pushes against it. "No! You will pay for this insolence!" it roars, but the shadows are unraveling.

Calvin feels a surge of hope. "We can do this! Let's keep pushing!"

With every ounce of strength, they focus their energies, the light expanding and engulfing the shadows. Hayman feels the warmth of the Munchkins in his hands, their magic intertwining with his resolve.

"Light will always triumph over darkness!" he declares, and with that, they unleash a final burst of brilliance, driving the shadows into retreat.

As the darkness fades, the Heartwood glows brighter than ever, the trees standing tall and proud. The air shimmers with magic, and the oppressive weight of fear lifts.

"We did it!" Hayman exclaims, joy flooding through him. "The light of the Munchkins and our unity drove them away!"

But deep down, they know the battle is not over. They have won this confrontation, but the shadows will not rest for long. They will need to prepare for what is to come and seek the wisdom of the Council to ensure the safety of Gold Valley and everyone within it.

Chapter Nineteen
What Now?

As night settles over the forest, the six of them gather around a crackling fire, the warmth casting flickering shadows on their faces. The glow of the flames dances in the dark, creating a sense of safety amid the uncertainty that looms over them.

Calvin, feeling the weight of the moment, looks around at his companions. "What happens now?" he asks, his voice steady but laced with concern. "We've pushed back the darkness, but we still need to find a way to protect the Heartwood and the Munchkins. And I… I need to get home."

The fawn stares into the fire, its expression thoughtful. "First, we must reach the Council of Elders in the city. They hold the knowledge and power necessary to help us understand the shadows' movements and how to counteract them."

Titan nods, his deep voice resonating in the quiet night. "The Council can provide guidance. If they unite, we'll have a stronger front against the darkness. But we must be prepared for their skepticism. Many have lost faith in the forest's magic."

Tinman adjusts his stance, his metal reflecting the firelight. "We'll need to present our evidence. The encounter with the shadow showed them the real threat. If we can convey the urgency of our situation, they may be compelled to act.

Calvin's heart races at the thought of facing the Council. "And what about the Munchkins? They need our protection too. Can we bring them along, or will that draw more shadows?"

"The Munchkins are vital," the fawn replies. "Their light is a beacon of hope, and their magic is tied to the Heartwood. We must ensure they are safe and ready to help when needed."

The group falls into a contemplative silence, each person lost in their thoughts. Calvin looks at the fire, its flames flickering like the possibilities ahead. "I know we've faced a lot already, but I believe in us. Together, we can make a difference."

"Exactly," Titan says, his voice firm. "We're stronger together. Tomorrow, we'll set out for the city and prepare to meet the Council. We can't let fear or doubt hold us back."

As the fire crackles and pops, they share stories of their past, laughter mingling with the warmth of the flames, strengthening their bonds. The night feels less daunting with the camaraderie they have built.

Eventually, as the stars twinkle overhead, Calvin feels a sense of resolve. Whatever challenges lie ahead, they will face them together, united by their purpose—to protect Gold Valley, the Munchkins, and ultimately, find a way for him to return home.

Chapter Twenty
The City

As dawn breaks, the first rays of sunlight filter through the trees, casting a warm glow over the forest.

Calvin feels a mix of excitement and anxiety as they prepare to leave for the city. Today is a crucial step in their journey.

"Let's move quickly," Titan urges, his voice steady. "We need to reach the city before the shadows can regroup."

They set off, navigating through the dense underbrush, the fawn leading the way. The path winds through the forest, and as they walk, the atmosphere shifts. The air feels charged with anticipation as if the forest itself is holding its breath for what lies ahead.

After hours of travel, they finally emerge from the trees, and before them lie the sprawling expanse of the city. Towering walls made of ancient stone surrounded it, covered in vines and blooming flowers that whispered of the magic within. The city shimmered under the sunlight, a blend of natural beauty and crafted architecture.

Calvin can't help but gasp. "It's incredible," he murmurs, taking in the sight. "I've never seen anything like it."

The fawn nods, eyes wide with wonder. "This is Emerald City, the heart of our realm. But we must remain cautious; not all within the city are friendly."

Calvin takes a moment to absorb the fawn's warning as they step deeper into the bustling streets. Colorful banners flutter in the breeze, and the air is filled with the sounds of laughter and chatter. Yet, beneath the vibrancy, there is an undercurrent of tension that makes him uneasy.

"What do you mean by that?" Calvin asks, glancing around. "Are there factions in the city?"

"Yes," the fawn replies, its expression serious. "While many wish to protect the forest and its magic, others are more concerned with their power and interests. Some may even see the shadows as an opportunity to gain control."

Titan growls softly, a low rumble in his throat. "We must tread carefully then. If there are those who would exploit the chaos, we need to be vigilant."

They continue through the winding streets, passing merchants selling vibrant wares, street performers captivating onlookers, and citizens going about their daily lives. But Calvin notices some glances directed their way—curious, wary, even hostile. It is clear they don't belong here.

"We should find the Council Hall quickly," Tinman suggests, his eyes scanning the crowd for any signs of trouble. "The sooner we get to the Council, the sooner we can address the threat."

Chapter Twenty-One
The Elders

As they approach the grand building, Calvin feels a mix of hope and anxiety. The Council Hall towers above them, and its architecture is a testament to the city's rich history. The entrance is adorned with intricate carvings of past heroes and battles fought for the realm's safety.

"Here we are," the fawn says, leading them up the steps. "Remember, we need to present our case clearly. The Elders must understand the urgency."

Inside, the hall is vast and echoing, sunlight streaming through high windows, illuminating the assembly of Elders seated in a semicircle. Their eyes are sharp, assessing the newcomers.

Calvin steps forward, heart pounding. "We seek your counsel. The darkness threatens the Heartwood and the Munchkins. We need your help to unite against this threat."

One of the Elders, a wise-looking figure with a long beard, raises an eyebrow. "And what proof do you bring of this darkness?"

Hayman produces the small Munchkin, its gentle glow filling the space. "This Munchkin is a living testament to the threat we face.

It is tied to the Heartwood and in danger. The shadows have already attacked us."

The Elders lean closer, their skepticism beginning to wane as they see the glowing creature. Murmurs ripple through the assembly, and Calvin seizes the moment.

"We need to act quickly. The shadows are growing bolder, and if we do not unite the city, the darkness will consume everything we hold dear," he implores, feeling the urgency of their situation.

The lead Elder studies them for a long moment, then speaks, "If what you say is true, then we must consider our options. But know this: many here have lost faith in the forest's magic and may not be easily swayed."

Calvin's heart sinks slightly at the thought of convincing the city. "We can show them the truth. If we gather allies and demonstrate the strength of our unity, we can protect the Heartwood and the Munchkins."

Titan steps forward, his voice firm. "We must rally the citizens. If they see the threat for themselves, they will understand the need for action."

The Council exchanges glances, their expressions contemplative. The weight of their decision hangs in the air, and Calvin feels the moment stretches into eternity. This is their chance to bring the light back to Gold Valley — and perhaps to find a way home for Calvin.

The lead Elder nods slowly. "Very well. We will hear your case and decide how to proceed. But know that your words must be backed by action. We must gather the citizens and present a united front against the shadows."

Calvin feels a rush of hope. "Thank you. We'll do whatever it takes."

As they prepare to address the city, he knows the path ahead will be fraught with challenges, but with their newfound allies and the light of the Munchkins, they have a chance to stand against the darkness together.

As the group leaves the Elders, a mix of determination and anxiety settles over them. The Council has agreed to consider their plea, but now it is up to them to gather proof of the dark shadows' threat to present to the citizens of Emerald City.

"Where do we start?" Calvin asks, glancing at his companions as they step into the bustling streets again.

"We need to find witnesses," the fawn suggests, its ears twitching with urgency. "Others who have seen the shadows or experienced their attacks firsthand."

Titan nods. "We can split up to cover more ground. Some of us can search for villagers who might have stories to share, while others can look for any signs of the darkness in the area."

"Good idea," Tinman replies, his metal glinting in the sunlight. "I'll go with you, Calvin. We can check the market for anyone who might have encountered the shadows."

"Hayman and I can explore the outskirts of the city," the fawn says. "Those who live closer to the forest might have seen or heard something."

Calvin feels a rush of excitement. "Let's meet back here in a couple of hours. We'll share what we find and come up with a plan to present our evidence to the Council and the citizens."

Chapter Twenty-Two
Seeking Witnesses

As they split up, Calvin and Tinman make their way toward the bustling market square. The atmosphere is lively, with vendors calling out to passersby and children playing in the streets. Yet beneath the surface, Calvin senses an undercurrent of tension — whispers about strange occurrences and shadows lurking just beyond the city walls.

"Stay alert," Tinman cautions as they approach a group of villagers huddled near a stall. "We're looking for anyone who might have seen the shadows."

Calvin nods, his heart racing as they near the villagers. "Excuse me," he calls out, trying to sound confident. "We are gathering information about strange happenings in the area. Has anyone seen anything unusual lately?"

A woman with worried eyes steps forward. "You mean those dark figures? Yes, I saw them creeping near the edge of the forest last week. They moved like smoke, but there was something… sinister about them."

Calvin's pulse quickens. "Did you see anyone get hurt?"

The woman shakes her head, but her voice trembles. "Not directly. But I heard whispers of others who've had encounters, friends. It's not safe out there anymore."

Tinman leans in, his tone serious. "Can you describe what you saw? Any details might help us."

The woman nods, her gaze shifting nervously. "They seem to drain the light around them. I felt cold like the warmth of the sun had disappeared. It was as if they thrived in darkness."

Calvin exchanges a glance with Tinman, sensing they are on the right track. "Thank you. This is vital information."

As they continue to ask questions, more villagers share their stories, each account weaving a clearer picture of the shadows that threaten their realm. They note the chilling cold, the sudden darkness, and the feelings of despair that go with the shadows' presence.

After gathering several accounts, Calvin feels a sense of urgency. "We should meet back with the others," he says to Tinman. "We need to compile everything we've learned and figure out how to present it."

The two make their way back to the Council Hall, the weight of their discoveries heavy on their shoulders. When they arrive, they find Hayman and the fawn already waiting, their expressions a mix of determination and concern.

"Did you find anything?" Hayman asks, his eyes bright with curiosity.

"More than we expected," Calvin replies, sharing the stories they have gathered. "The shadows are real, and people are scared. We have proof of their presence, and we need to present this to the Council."

As they discuss their findings, the urgency of their mission settles in. They will face the Council again, armed with firsthand accounts and the strength of their unity. With the light of the Munchkins and the resolve of the forest at their backs, they are ready to confront the darkness together.

Chapter Twenty-Three
The Proof

The atmosphere in the Council Hall is tense as Calvin and his companions prepare to present their findings. The Elders are seated in their semicircle, their expressions serious and expectant. The flickering light from the torches cast shadows across the room, a stark reminder of the very threat they face.

Calvin steps forward, heart pounding. "Thank you for allowing us to return," he begins, gathering his thoughts. "We've gathered evidence of the dark shadows that are threatening our home and the Heartwood."

Hayman steps up beside him, holding a small Munchkin that glows softly. "This is one of the last remaining Munchkins, a symbol of hope and light. Its magic is intertwined with the Heartwood, and it's in grave danger."

Calvin takes a deep breath, feeling the weight of his words. "We spoke to the villagers, and they shared their experiences — accounts of shadows creeping near the forest, draining the light and warmth from the surroundings."

He glances at Tinman, who nods and steps forward with a notebook filled with notes. "Here are the testimonies we collected." He opens the book, reading aloud from it. "One villager described a chilling encounter: 'It was like a cold mist moving through the trees, whispering threats. I felt my hope fading with the light.'"

The Elders listen intently, their expressions shifting from skepticism to concern. Calvin continues, recounting other stories of despair, fear, and the unsettling darkness that has begun to encroach upon their lives.

"The shadows are not just a threat to the forest," he concludes. "They are a threat to all of us. If we do not unite and act now, they will consume everything."

The lead Elder, who has still been silent until now, speaks up. "Your accounts are troubling. But we need more than stories to rally the city. We need to show the citizens the reality of this threat."

Calvin nods, understanding the gravity of the situation. "What if we organize a demonstration? We can bring the villagers who saw the shadows to speak. If the citizens hear their accounts firsthand, they might see the truth in what we're saying."

The Elders exchange glances, considering the proposal. "This could work," the lead Elder says slowly. "But we must ensure it is done safely. We cannot put anyone at risk."

"I can help with that," the fawn offers. "I'll gather the villagers and bring them here for the demonstration. We need to ensure that as many citizens as possible understand the urgency of our situation."

Titan nods. "And we can patrol the perimeter to keep an eye out for any signs of the shadows during the gathering."

With a plan beginning to form, the atmosphere in the hall shifts from uncertainty to determination. Calvin feels a surge of hope. "Let's set this in motion. The sooner we act, the better."

As they begin organizing the demonstration, Calvin's thoughts race. He can't shake the feeling that the shadows are still lurking, waiting for the right moment to strike. But he knows they have to act—united, with the light of the Munchkins guiding them.

Hours later, the sun begins to dip below the horizon, casting a warm glow over Emerald City. The citizens gather, curiosity and concern etched on their faces as they make their way to the Council Hall. Calvin stands with his companions at the front, their resolve steeled for what lies ahead.

As the villagers arrive, Hayman takes a deep breath. "Let's show them the truth. Together."

One by one, the villagers step forward to share their experiences. Their voices tremble with emotion as they recount their encounters with the shadows—how the air had turned icy, how whispers of despair had filled their ears, and how they had felt the very light being siphoned from their surroundings.

The crowd listens, captivated, and horrified. Calvin feels the weight of their collective fear and hope as they begin to understand the reality of the threat.

Then, as the final villagers finish their account, a sudden chill sweeps through the air. The firelight flickers ominously, casting long shadows that dance along the walls. Calvin exchanges worried glances with his friends.

"We need to remain vigilant," Titan warns, his eyes scanning the perimeter.

And just as he speaks, a dark mist begins to creep into the square, coiling around the edges like a living thing. Gasps ripple through the crowd as the shadows begin to take form, swirling ominously.

Calvin's heart races. "It's here! We need to protect everyone!"

With urgency, the group rallies together, ready to confront the darkness head-on. The time for proof has arrived, and they are determined to stand against the encroaching shadows, united in their fight for the light.

Chapter Twenty-Four
It Appears

The dark mist coalesces before them, twisting, and writhing until it takes the shape of a massive wolf, its eyes glowing like embers in the night. The very air around it seems to chill, an oppressive darkness radiating from its form. Calvin's heart sinks as recognition washes over him.

"It's the same wolf!" he exclaims, stepping back instinctively. "The one that attacked Heyman and I on our journey!"

The crowd gasps, fear rippling through them. The wolf's growl resonates deeply, a sound that sends shivers down Calvin's spine. It prowls forward, its shadowy body shifting and swirling, as if it is made of smoke and night.

"We mustn't let it scare us!" the fawn shouts, standing tall despite the fear in its eyes. "This is the manifestation of the darkness we've been talking about! We need to stand together!"

Calvin feels a surge of courage. He remembers the warmth of the Munchkins and the power of unity that brought them this far. "Everyone, gather close!" he calls out, raising the glowing Munchkin high. "We need to focus our light!"

As the villagers huddle together, the Munchkins' glow intensifies, illuminating the square. The Elders step forward, their wisdom guiding their actions. "We will not be intimidated by shadows!" the lead Elder declares, lifting his staff. "We stand for the light of the forest!"

The wolf snarls, its eyes narrowing as the light pushes against its darkness. It lunges forward, but Calvin and his friends stand firm, channeling their energy into the Munchkin. The light expands, swirling around them like a protective barrier.

"Focus on the light!" Hayman shouts, the Munchkins in their pockets responding, glowing brighter in response to their collective will. "Together, we can drive it back!"

With a united shout, they direct the light at the wolf, and it howls in fury as the brightness strikes it. The shadows around it flicker and thin, revealing hints of its true form—an embodiment of fear and despair.

The wolf staggers, the glow pushing it back, but it isn't finished yet. With a powerful leap, it lunges toward Calvin, teeth bared, darkness swirling around it. Calvin braces himself, fear surging through him, but he remembers the warmth of his friends beside him.

"Now!" Calvin shouts, and together, they unleash the full power of the Munchkins. A brilliant beam of light shoots forth, enveloping the wolf in a radiant embrace. It howls once more, a sound that echoes through the night, resonating with the fear and darkness it represents.

The shadows begin to peel away, unraveling from the wolf's form like smoke dissipating in the wind. With each pulse of light from the Munchkins, the dark essence that comprised the creature trembles, revealing glimpses of its true nature. As the darkness lifts, it morphs, twisting and reshaping until it takes on the familiar form of the old lady who lived in the cottage—a figure Calvin had seen before, the old lady was now free from the wolf's form, still harbored a dark presence deep inside her—one that seems intent on destroying all that was pure in Gold Valley and the Heartwood. Just as then, a chilling scream pierces the air, echoing from the depths of the shadows that still cling to her.

The sound is unmistakable: the terrified screams of three little girls.

Calvin's heart drops. "What was that?" he shouts, urgency flooding his voice. "Who's screaming?"

The old lady's eyes widen in horror, a flicker of recognition crossing her face. "No… not them! I thought I had protected them!"

As the shadows twist and surge around her, they coalesce into a darker, more menacing form — an embodiment of the fears that have tormented her for so long. The screams grow louder, more desperate, filling the square with an eerie dread.

"Stay back!" the fawn calls, stepping forward protectively. "We need to confront whatever is inside her! It's trying to take control!"

The Elders raise their staff, preparing to summon the light once more, but Calvin feels a surge of resolve. "We have to help her! We can't let the darkness win!"

"Calvin, be careful!" Tinman warns, his metal frame tense. But Calvin doesn't hesitate; he steps closer to the old lady, his heart racing.

"Listen to me!" he shouts, trying to reach her through the chaos. "You have to fight this! Those girls are counting on you!"

The shadows around the old lady writhe violently, the screams intensifying, as if the darkness is battling against her will. "I'm so sorry! I couldn't protect them!" she cries, tears streaming down her face. "The darkness…it's too strong!"

"Channel the love you have for them!" Calvin urges, his voice steady. "Remember their laughter, the moments you shared! That light is still within you!"

The shadows hesitate, flickering as if torn between consuming her and retreating. Calvin sees a glimmer of light in the old lady's eyes as she struggles against the darkness. "I can't let it take them! I have to save them!" she shouts, her voice fierce with newfound determination.

With a sudden burst of energy, the old lady reaches deep within herself, drawing forth the remnants of her light, igniting a spark of hope amidst the encroaching darkness. The shadows recoil, momentarily stunned by the power of her love.

"Together!" Calvin cries, turning back to the villagers. "Everyone, focus your light! Let's push back the darkness!"

The villagers rally, the Munchkins glowing brighter than ever as they direct their energy toward the old lady. The air fills with warmth, pushing against the shadows that encircle her. The old lady closes her eyes, her voice rising above the chaos. "I won't let you take them!"

With that declaration, the dark presence surrounding her begins to unravel, the screams of the little girls morphing into soft, echoing whispers. As the light intensifies, the shadows split apart, revealing the three girls—lost but not gone, their forms ethereal and shimmering.

They call, their voices fill with fear and longing.

"Hold on! I'm coming!" the old lady shouts, reaching out toward them. The light swirls around her, lifting her, and pushing the darkness back.

The girls begin to glow, their innocence illuminating the shadows that have threatened to consume them. "We're here! We're safe!" they cry, and the darkness recoils in terror, its grip loosening as the light overwhelms it.

In a final surge, the villagers focus all their energy on the Munchkins, a radiant beam shooting forth and enveloping the old lady and the girls. The dark essence shatters, dissolving into a cascade of shimmering sparks.

As the last of the shadows vanishes, the three little girls stand before the crowd, unharmed and glowing with the light of the Munchkins. The old lady collapses to her knees, tears of relief streaming down her face as she embraces them tightly.

"I thought I lost you," she whispers, her voice breaking with emotion. The girls hug her back, their laughter mingling with the cheers of the villagers.

Calvin looks around, filled with awe at the power of their unity and the resilience of love. They have faced the darkness together and emerged stronger.

"Let this be a lesson for us all," the lead Elder declares, stepping forward. "When we stand together, we can overcome even the deepest and darkest shadows."

Chapter Twenty-Five
Triumph

As the villagers celebrate, Calvin feels a renewed sense of hope. They have not only saved the old lady and the girls but have also shown that love and unity can triumph over the darkest fears. The light of Gold Valley is shining brighter than ever, and together, they will continue to protect it.

Yet, with all that the town has been through, one thing remains heavy on Calvin's mind: how much he misses his beloved dog and his family. As the townspeople celebrate their victory over the dark shadow, laughter, and joy filling the air, Calvin stands apart from the festivities, feeling a sense of emptiness amidst the triumph.

He watches as the old lady embraces her daughters, their reunion a beautiful sight that tugs at his heart. Memories of his own family flash through his mind—the sound of his dog's joyful barks, the warmth of his mother's hugs, and the laughter shared around the dinner table. The stark contrast between their joy and his own longing makes the celebration bittersweet.

Calvin sighs, gazing up at the stars beginning to twinkle in the dusk sky. "I should be with them," he murmurs to himself, feeling the weight of his absence more than ever. The battle against the darkness has been won, but the shadows of his own heart loom large.

The fawn notices Calvin's distant expression and approaches him. "You, okay?" it asked, concern etched on its face.

Calvin forces a smile but shakes his head. "I'm just… I miss my dog. And my family. This place is amazing, but I can't shake the feeling of being so far away from home."

The fawn nods, understanding the ache of separation. "Home is important. It gives us strength. But remember, you're not alone. We're all in this together now."

"Yeah," Calvin replies softly, appreciating the fawn's words. "But I still feel lost."

Just then, Hayman joins them, with a beaming smile on his face. "Calvin! You should come and join the celebration! Everyone wants to thank you for what you did. You helped us face our fears!"

"I know, but…" Calvin hesitates, glancing back at the joyful crowd. "I can't help but feel like something's missing."

Hayman looks thoughtful for a moment. "Maybe it's not about what's missing, but what you can create here. This place is starting to feel like home for many of us, including you."

Calvin considers this the idea sparking a flicker of hope. "You're right. I can't ignore my feelings, but maybe I can find a way to connect with this place while I search for a way back home."

The fawn perks up. "And we can help! We're a community now. We can work together to find a way to help you get back to your family and your dog."

As the celebration continues, Calvin feels a shift within himself. He joins Hayman and the fawn, weaving through the crowd, accepting the gratitude and warmth of the townspeople. Their smiles and laughter begin to lift the heaviness in his heart, and he realizes he has the support of new friends in this strange land.

With each interaction, Calvin feels more rooted in the present, while still keeping a piece of his longing for home close. Perhaps he can honor his family by being the light in this community, just as they have always been for him.

As night falls and the stars twinkle overhead, Calvin takes a deep breath. "Alright, let's celebrate. I may not be home yet, but I can find joy here, too. And I won't stop searching for a way back."

The fawn nods enthusiastically. "That's the spirit! Together, we'll figure it out!"

With renewed determination, Calvin joined the festivities, allowing the warmth of friendship and community to fill the void.

He might be far from home, but in that moment, surrounded by laughter and light, he felt a glimmer of hope for both his journey and the adventure that lay ahead.